A IS FOR ANGELICA

Gordon Kingdom struggles with the fate of his seriously-ill wife while observing and methodically recording the lives of those around him: his neighbours. He has files on them all, including Don Donald (best friend and petty thief), Annie Carnaffan (lives next door, throws footballs over the fence), and Benny (the boy who paints with his eyes closed). And then there's Angelica, the new girl on the street, with her multi-coloured toenails and her filthy temper. It's when she arrives that Gordon's world of half-truths begins to unravel. Faced with a series of unexpected events and a faltering conscience, he's left with an impossible decision . . .

IAIN BROOME

A IS FOR ANGELICA

Complete and Unabridged

ULVERSCROFT
Leicester

First published in Great Britain in 2012 by
Legend Press Ltd.
London

First Large Print Edition
published 2014
by arrangement with
Legend Press Ltd.
London

A catalogue record for this book is available
from the British Library.

ISBN 978–1–4448–1818–5

Published by
F. A. Thorpe (Publishing)
Anstey, Leicestershire

Set by Words & Graphics Ltd.
Anstey, Leicestershire
Printed and bound in Great Britain by
T. J. International Ltd., Padstow, Cornwall

This book is printed on acid-free paper

For Suzy

Some thank yous

My family, for all their love and support. The Whites, for all their love and support too. My friends, for their love, support and gentle ribbing. Simon Crump, for setting me off on the right path and for demonstrating the art of editing with the use of an actual axe (murder your darlings). Alex Moody, for providing the space for me to realise that writing a novel was going to be really, really hard work. And for the cricket. Obviously. Sophie Lambert, for her advice, guidance and unique ability to say exactly the right thing at exactly the right time.

And Suzy, for her love, patience, and unwavering faith in me and *Angelica*.

Angelica

If I look hard enough, it will go away.

So I sit and I stare.

This morning I prayed for forgiveness.

It's evening now. The sky through the window tapers up from the rooftops, red to blue, blue to black. I'm on a chair with a cushion tied to the seat. I moved it from the kitchen nearly a year ago. It doesn't belong there anymore. It's just the chair by the bed that no-one else sits on. It gives me backache. A strip of light shines through from the landing. I think about it waking her up, hurting her eyes should they open. I imagine I'm someone else looking in through the window from across the street, watching this room faintly lit by the glow of another. I hope someone sees me, follows the light through the gap in the door and writes down what I'm about to do.

Angelica walks in. She offers me a piece of chocolate cake.

'Have you finished?' she says. 'It's almost time.' I don't answer properly. I never answer properly. I sit and I stare.

'Did you know the Russians have a special

word for light blue?'

She looks away. Sips her tea. Shakes her head.

'Just get on with it,' she replies. 'Before your drink gets cold.'

Benny

Benny paints pictures with his eyes closed. I keep a thick file on Benny. He paints every day between one and two in the morning and his light is always the last in the street to go out. It would be mine, but I never switch it on when I'm in the spare room, adding to a file. It's easy to write in the dark. My eyes have nothing to adjust to, or from.

Last summer, Benny became the youngest ever nominee for the Harris Manning Arts Award. It was in the local papers. A picture of him shaking hands with the mayor. He sold three of his paintings for £2000, which is far too much money to give a sixteen-year-old boy. He was in the papers for that as well, this time with his arm around an art collector from London. Benny's mother, Jenny, was standing next to him. She was holding an oversized cheque. I cut the picture out and put it with the others.

★   ★   ★

I can see into Benny's room. He has a row of five candles lined up along the windowsill. He

3

lights them when he's painting. His window doesn't have curtains because he set fire to them. When he paints, the back of his canvas always faces the street. I've watched him painting for hours, but I've never seen one of his pictures. They never put Benny's pictures in the papers — just pictures of Benny.

When he lights his candles, I can see the air around the flames shimmering, like when roads get hot in summer. The candles illuminate half the room. Benny disappears, flicks the switch by the door, comes back through the half-light like a ghost. He stands at his easel and picks up the paintbrush, holds it stretched in front of him, leans forward until it touches the canvas, arches his neck, lifts his head and closes his eyes. He opens them again when he's done, when there's air between his picture and the paintbrush.

I started Benny's file a year ago, the day of the fire. I sat on the end of the bed in the spare room, looking out through the window at an empty street. A row of closed curtains, darkness behind darkness. His curtains were thick enough to hide the light from the candles; close enough to catch the heat from the flames. They ate the material from the bottom up. I began to see Benny, the tops of his legs, then his stomach. He was perfectly still, revealed like the opening of a play.

And then there was movement. A paint-brush fell to the floor, the curtains opened and closed as Benny pulled and yanked them from the rail. I watched him jumping up and down, trying to put the fire out, the flames dancing across his bedroom floor, the only light in the street. Then it rose again. It hovered in the air, just for a second, and then tumbled out into the night. Benny sat on his bed in a tangle of shades, black and blacker still. A room framed like a picture, only outlines of objects to go by.

I picked up my pen and started writing.

Note: Benny Martin has an easel in his room. He set fire to his curtains and threw them out of the window. Time for fire to die = 32 minutes. Note end.

I see Benny twice a day. Once when he leaves for school in the morning and again at night when he's painting. I never see him come back because he enters the house through the back door. John Bonsall told me so. He can see him from his kitchen, climbing over the wall and into the back garden. Benny wears the same jacket every day. It's a navy suit jacket with three badges attached to the right lapel. The badges change colour each morning. He collects them. His hair is long around his ears. Sometimes he ties it into a ponytail with a light blue band. I remember him being born in the back of his mother's Mini Metro. She wasn't driving. His father was. Before the divorce. They were on their way to hospital, but she couldn't hold on. It ruined the upholstery.

When Benny was a child he played football on his own in the street. He'd wear trousers with holes in, dribble around the parked cars and kick the ball against my fence. Sometimes I'd go out and watch him, shout encouragement from the garden. He'd ask me to join in, but I'd always tell him he was far too good for me. He'd carry on regardless, dribbling and kicking, happy as Larry. One day, while he was playing, a dog pulled free from its owner and sank its teeth into Benny's leg. It refused to let go. He never played again.

I haven't spoken to Benny since he was twelve-years-old. Apart from once. It was two years ago. I was walking home from church. I'd been in early with some leaflets from the neighbourhood watch. As I turned into the street, I saw Benny leaving his house to go to school. He walked towards me with his bag over his shoulder. His jacket had one green, one orange and one red badge attached, like upside down traffic lights. His limp seemed worse than usual.

'Good morning,' I said, as he got near.

'What are you looking at?' he replied, and carried on walking.

Birthdays

It's the day after New Year's Day, and it's my birthday. Kipling, my dog, has diarrhoea. This means I haven't taken him for his eight o'clock march to the dog mess bin. To use it you have to put your hand inside a plastic sandwich bag, pick up the mess and turn the bag inside out. You carry the bag to the bin. It's a trusted technique, but not for me. Not anymore. Not since I bought the wrong sandwich bags, the ones with two holes in the bottom to ventilate the food. I've developed a technique of my own. I time it so that Kipling gets to the bin at exactly the right moment. Then I pick him up, cut out the middleman.

Note: 7.15 a.m. feed Kipling. 8.00 a.m. take Kipling for walk. Judge speed of walk on food left in Kipling's bowl. 8.15 a.m. to 8.30 a.m. (varies) arrive at dog mess bin. Estimated saving on sandwich bags = 28 pence. Risk factor = 6. Note end.

There's a woman walking towards me from across the road. She's smiling and waving a pair of scissors in the air. I don't know who she is. I've never seen her before. She has long black hair tied back in a ponytail and she's wearing a pair of tight fitting jeans with coloured cotton embroidered around the hem: pink, purple, orange and black. The sleeve of her cardigan falls away from her shoulder as she bounces over the kerb. I can see part of her upper arm. Thin with faint creases, like the lines on her neck when she smiles. I stare at her. And then I remember, Kipling's diarrhoea. She goes to speak to me. Her eyes are green and twinkling and I have my hand in an inside out sandwich bag, holding a soggy log of dog mess.

'Hello, my name's Angelica,' she says. 'I've just moved into twenty-three.' A pair of yellow Marigold gloves half-hang out the back pockets of her jeans. Some of the fingers are inside out.

'I'm Gordon Kingdom,' I reply. She nods at me and smiles. 'I live on this side of the road. On your side you've got Ina Macaukey. She's at twenty-five and not long out of hospital. Next to her is Morris Webster and Ginger at twenty-seven. Ginger's a cat. You'll not see much of them. Then there's the Martins at twenty-one. The rest you can work out for yourself.'

'It sounds like a friendly place.'

'And like I say, I live here, number

eighteen. On this side.'

'I see,' she says, looking at me. She thinks I haven't finished, that there's more to come. There's an uncomfortable pause between us and I notice how pretty she must have been, at some point. Her cheeks are flushed red, from the cold I think, though they might be her normal-coloured cheeks. Now she's staring at the inside out bag of dog mess in my hand. She can't be a day over forty-two. Ten years younger than me.

'My dog's not well. He's been sick in the house. I couldn't walk him this morning.'

'I see,' she says again, still smiling. I should leave it at that.

'He's shit on the bathroom floor as well. By the time I get in, he'll have probably shit on the landing.'

Now she's staring, not smiling. Her jacket has opened slightly at the top. She's wearing a bright yellow v-neck underneath. The colour matches the gloves in her pockets. I see the slightest centimetre of cleavage, a smidgeon, an ounce. And I can't believe she made me say shit. Twice.

'So how's the house?' I ask.

'It's fine. Empty though. The van's coming this afternoon. I just brought a few boxes over in the car.'

'Where is it?'

'The van?'

'No, the car.'

'Oh, it wasn't mine.'

There's another uncomfortable pause. Her ponytail sways because she's slowly shifting her weight from one foot to the other. She must be cold.

'So, how's the house?' I ask.

'You just asked me that.'

'Yes. Sorry. Is there anything else you want to know?'

'Not really. Who am I replacing?'

'What do you mean?'

'Who lived here before me?'

'Karen Carpenter.'

'Really? *The* Karen Carpenter?'

'No. This one was Welsh.'

'Did she live on her own?'

'No. She lived with a husband.'

'Well, I'm only renting at the moment.'

'So were they. For fifteen years.'

'Why did they leave?'

'I think they found somewhere better.'

'I see,' she says. And then we stop again, just long enough for her to have legitimate grounds to say, 'Well I'd better get on with it, get it finished before the van arrives,' and for me to reply, 'Of course, I'd better let you go.'

I watch her turn and walk away. She looks

younger from behind. Slimmer. She opens her front door.

'It's my birthday!' I shout.

She turns and shouts back, 'Mine too!'

'You're joking!'

'No! Happy Birthday!'

She's joking. She has to be. But either way, I don't mind, so I shout, 'Happy birthday to you too!' and crouch behind the garden fence where she can't see me. As if I'd been down here beforehand. I look at the dog mess in my hand, squeezing into shapes inside the bag. I think I hear her shout something else. Then a door closing. I stand up and she's gone.

★　★　★

It snowed this afternoon. I watched the flakes settle on the grass, cars and pavement as I opened a new folder, filed Angelica under A. Now it's dark and there's a veil of white draped across the street like a just-washed tablecloth. I take Angelica's file and make notes about our conversation this morning. I write s*** instead of shit and try to describe the way she walked across the road, both towards and away from me. Her small steps and folded arms. Scissors poking out of her back pocket.

At half past midnight, I put her file back

Cressington Vale

I hid behind curtains before I met Angelica.

It started the day I caught the vicar's wife masturbating with the blinds open, her full-length mirror tipped at an unfortunate angle. In truth, he's not really a vicar and she's not really his wife. He's a Jehovah's Witness. She's his bit on the side. I thought about slipping a note discreetly under the door to stop it happening again, but I decided against it. Besides, she should've known better. She's older than me. After that, I found myself sitting by the window for hours on end, surveying the street. Letting the world drift past. Taking my mind off things. I watched my neighbours and got to know them better than I ever had before. Their changes in behaviour. Their simplest of movements. Their finest of details.

These are skills that I've developed. I never kept watch when I was young. But I listened hard and heard everything. Like the things my friends would say when they thought I'd left the room. And my parents having intercourse. I only heard them once, but the worry stopped me sleeping. I made

nightly interventions, which included coughing loudly and walking to the bathroom to
flush the toilet. Anything to let them know
that I was there and still awake. Anything to
stop it. Sometimes one of them would get up
and come to my room. They'd ask me what
was wrong and I'd tell them I'd had
nightmares. This went on for over a year, until
my mother said she was going to take me to
the doctor. So I told her the truth. She was
silent for more than fifteen seconds. Then she
laughed quietly and rubbed her eyes to show
me that she was tired. 'Your mum and dad
both love each other,' she said by way of
explanation. As if that changed a thing.

I listened hard at work too, when things
were different. When I had a job to go to, an
office to work in and meetings to attend. But
those things are gone. Cressington Vale is my
office now. It's better than a real job. There
are no conversations with colleagues who are
younger than me, who feign interest in my
weekends. No sitting at a desk, watching
through a gap in a blind as they leave early to
drink together. No listening to other people's
conversations through thin, fabricated walls.
No waiting for someone else to do his or her
job properly so that I can do mine. There's
none of this. These are things that used to
happen. These are things that will never

happen again. My life is different now. I don't go to work. I don't have an office. I stay at home, hide behind curtains and make notes. I wait for something to happen.

For example, the average bay window for a house on Cressington Vale is approximately three and a half feet from the floor, so when someone sits in their front room to watch the television, or eat their dinner on a tray, I only see them from the neck up. Each day I make a list of the time each head-in-the-window becomes a body and gets up to close the curtains. Ina Macaukey is always the last. She sits and crochets in the light from her television. Its colours always changing. When all the curtains are closed, I make supper, read the newspaper or go upstairs and sit by the spare room window. That's where all the action is. It's where I keep my files. I can see up and down the street, over the trees in the road and occasionally into bedrooms. I avert my eyes at the slightest sign of nakedness. I'm never indiscreet. But there have been incidences. First there was the 'vicar's wife', and then the unpleasantness of glimpsing a penis at number nineteen. I turned away, but not quickly enough to avoid registering the offending member as not belonging to Peter Smith, as perhaps I might have expected, what with his wife, Janice, closing the downstairs curtains just half an hour before. I never say anything though. These matters are not my business. Not any more.

I used to be part of the neighbourhood watch committee. I was watch coordinator for fifteen years, six months and twenty-five days, appointed following a spate of muggings in the local area and around six weeks after the previous coordinator resigned. She'd been one of the victims. Before then I'd been watch secretary. My responsibilities included planning meetings and taking minutes. I also set up and provided a reminder service, where I would ring committee members approximately three hours prior to a meeting. I'd let the phone ring twice and then hang up. To track attendance I created spreadsheets, which I ruled out by hand and completed in pencil, then traced the lines with a thin marker.

These days there is no neighbourhood watch. In fact sometimes it feels like I'm the only one who does any watching at all. Cressington Vale is a quiet street and one of the oldest in town, tucked away from the new housing estates. But misdemeanours take place on quiet streets. They still need rules and boundaries. So I keep a file labelled 'Suspicious behaviour', which I add to almost every other day. It's a dossier of unusual happenings. Most involve neighbours. Like when Andrea Turner returned home late from work with a towel wrapped round her head. She'd been to her first aqua aerobics. Or when Don Donald, my oldest friend, left his mattress on the front lawn. He'd been bitten twenty-seven times in the night and only on his legs. He said he wanted to give it some air.

I've found that if you ask directly, people will explain themselves.

Cigarettes

Angelica has been here less than a week. She's changed everything. The snow has gone. I haven't made a single note on anyone else since she moved in, apart from Benny. I've still made notes on Benny, and I've still hidden behind curtains, but I've only been looking for her. Everything else seems incidental. Like two people speaking at once. Eventually one of them gets lost, drifts away.

Angelica lives on her own and smokes outside. She always smokes before she goes to bed. She's doing it now, sat on her doorstep. It's half past eleven. I'm watching her from the spare room. The night hides the colour of her clothes. I can see her perfectly clearly, but she's in several shades of grey. She takes long hard drags of her cigarette and blows smoke into the sky. I think about our conversation again. The day she moved in. The boxes in the street and Angelica marching with her scissors in her hand, ordering the removal men here, there and everywhere, mucking in, taking boxes into her hallway, putting them down, using her scissors to slice through the masking tape. She'd open a box, see what was inside and write on it with a marker pen, and I'd wonder why she hadn't done that when she packed. The removal men drove away at four o'clock when it was getting dark. Angelica sat slumped on her doorstep, same place she's sitting now. Her hair escaping from her ponytail, loose around her neck.

I'm going to go and speak to her.

What can I say?

I could tell her that the cake was from me.

She can see me coming.

She's going to speak first.

'Thanks for the cake. You shouldn't have gone to the trouble.'

'How did you know?'

'I didn't tell anyone else. And you should've knocked.'

'It was late.'

She leans back against the door. It comes ajar and she's in colour. Her toenails are painted, each one a different shade.

'Where's your husband?'

She leans forward again and the door closes. She's back in greyscale.

'I'm sorry?'

'You're wearing a ring.'

She folds her arms to hide the ring with her jumper. It's a huge jumper. It looks soft to touch.

'We're separated.'

21

'I see.'

I shouldn't have said it. I should have waited. I can feel my skin losing moisture. I'm sweating through my clothes and I can see the snap-twitch of Ina Macaukey's fingers out the corner of my eye. Her dark old face hung over her embroidery.

'Who's the boy that lives next door?' she asks.

'Benny. Benny Martin.'

'That's it. Benny. I knew I'd forget.'

She unfolds her arms and takes another drag from her cigarette. She does it smoothly, all in one movement. The grip, the inhalation and the release. One hand puts it in, the other takes it out. It looks even better close up.

'Why do you want to know about Benny? Have you seen him yet?'

'He helped me with some boxes.'

'I see. When?'

'Couple of days ago. He seems a nice boy.' I nod, she smiles.

'He was in the papers not long back.'

'Oh really? What for?'

'Stealing.'

'Seriously?' she says, like I'm lying.

'Yes, but it's all sorted now.'

'Well good. He seemed all right to me.'

'I'm sure he did. His mother is in the Women's Institute.'

'She seemed all right too.'

'You've met?'

'Of course.'

'Right. I see. She's only in her forties.'

'So am I, Gordon.'

Angelica stubs what's left of her cigarette out on the doorstep. She stands up, pushes the door open with her bare heel, and for the first time I notice that she's taller than me. Even without shoes. And now she's stepping inside the house. Our second conversation is ending and I still haven't thought of an opening line, my reason for speaking to her. My mind has gone blank.

'Is there anything else?' There is nothing else. I have nothing to say to her. I shouldn't be here anyway. I should be at home. I shake my head like a schoolchild. 'Good. Goodnight then,' she says, and turns away from me.

As the door closes, I whisper, 'Sleep tight,' and hope she doesn't hear me.

Then a voice comes from behind the door, 'Don't worry. I will.'

Note: Angelica's toenails far left to far right — 1 to 10 — red; yellow; turquoise; orange; red; red; orange; turquoise; yellow; red. Note end.

Next morning I get up, feed Kipling and take him for his walk. We get to the end of the street and he cocks his leg against his tree. He seems to be recovering. Cressington Vale has eight trees. Horse chestnuts. All of them growing through holes in the pavement, apart from one that grows out the road. It's always been like that. Cars have to wait for traffic coming the other way. Children swerve round it on their bikes. Hedgehogs get flattened. And Kipling urinates against it every day. It's his tree. I wait for him to finish and then we carry on walking, along Tickle Brook and up through the cemetery to the dog mess bin. Last night, I fell asleep writing in Angelica's file. I woke at seven this morning, fully-clothed and soaked in sweat. The spare room is a mess. There are papers everywhere. I'm going to tidy up when I get back, before Kipling treads on them or rips them to shreds. First job on the list. After that, I'll put him out in the back garden. Then I'm going to B&Q to find out how much chainsaws cost.

Don Donald

It's Don Donald. I owe him a jar of pickled onions.

'All right, Gordon? How are we?'

'We're fine, Don. How are you?'

'I'm good. Very well, in fact.'

Don Donald has lived on Cressington Vale all his life. His wife ran off with another man in 1984. He's been alone ever since. If I stand here long enough, he'll start talking about her. He'll tell me about her long blonde hair and her large chest. When she told him that she loved him. When he took her to the seafront in Blackpool, got down on one knee, asked her to be his wife. Then he'll say, 'Two weeks, Gordon. Two weeks and she'd gone.'

He tilts his head to one side. His face looks dirty, covered in folds and creases. He's trying to look sympathetic.

'So. How's things?'

'Things are fine, Don.'

'Everything going all right?'

'Going fine, Don. Things going all right with you?'

'Oh, very well.'

'That's good then,' I say, and think about

when we were younger. When we stood on this street and talked about the weather, or the football, or the chances of us ever getting the council to come and move the tree in the road. I think about when his wife first left. How I sat on a chair next to his bath while he lay in cold water for nine hours, talking and crying. I barely said a word. He didn't need me to.

'You should open your curtains, Gordon. Let the light in.'

'Where are my hedge trimmers?'

'I've no idea.'

'You borrowed them.' Don looks at the floor. Then at the sky. Then back at me again.

'Did I?'

'Yes, you did.'

'I'm sorry, Gordon. I don't remember.'

'I want them back.'

'I'm not sure I have them anymore.'

'I need them.' He takes his hands out the pockets of his pyjama bottoms and scratches his head.

'I can look for them.'

'Yes please.'

'All right then.' He stands there, puts his hands back in his pockets. I keep looking at him. 'You want me to find them now?'

'I need them.'

He turns, shuffles back across the road and

into his house. I hear the loose change in his pyjama pockets, his slippers scraping across the concrete. They sound like someone tearing paper.

Note: Cressington Vale = 14 paces wide. My garden = 10 paces. Don's drive = 12 paces (approx). Total = 36 paces. 36 paces = 40 seconds (approx). Note end.

I've tidied the spare room and made space on the bookcase for Angelica's file. Now I'm downstairs, behind the curtain, looking out for her. I'm also looking out for Don. It's almost one o'clock in the afternoon. He should have come back by now with my trimmers. It's a beautiful winter's day — freezing cold and bathed in sunshine. I look up at Angelica's bathroom window. Frosted glass. The sun reflecting. It leaves a neon circle in my field of vision, like a light bulb floating, which takes about a minute and a half to disappear. I watch the empty street. I have a notepad on the windowsill and a pen in my hand, but there is nothing for me to write. I have a headache. I need to make lunch. I squeeze the end of the pen to make the ballpoint disappear. I fold the notepad shut. As I turn away from the window, a door opens. Angelica? No, it's Ina Macaukey. She's bending over. She's picking up her milk. She's in her nightdress. I squeeze my pen again, flick through my notepad and check my watch. I scribble down the time.

Half an hour later, I walk to the kitchen and switch the kettle on. I take my watch off, place it on the worktop and roll up my sleeves. I turn the tap and rinse my hands, glance through the window. There's a football in my garden. Annie Carnaffan put it there. She throws them over the fence and at my kitchen window. She lives next door. She must be nearly ninety. I believe she does it on purpose, although I've never seen it happen, so I have no proof. I'm sure it's her. That's just the way she is, a nasty piece of work. I don't have a file on Annie Carnaffan. In fact, I don't have a file on anyone who lives on my side of Cressington Vale, because I can't see their windows. So I watch the opposite side of the street, where the action is. I make lists pages long. On anything and everything. And see the pattern of things, the way it all works. Systems and stability. Rhythms and recoveries. I have all these things on file. One file is thicker than the rest.

That file is for Georgina.

My wife.

Asleep upstairs.

Doctor Jonathan Morris

Doctor Morris is a suspected paedophile. I trust him completely.

He replaced Doctor Richmoor and this is his first practice. He's only twenty-eight-years-old and was accused of manhandling a thirteen-year-old girl within a fortnight of starting at the surgery. She said he'd pushed her against a wall and tried to lift her skirt up from behind. There were parents with placards for more than a week. It turned out she was pregnant and they disappeared. Because it's not like she hadn't been manhandled before. Doctor Morris was cleared a few days later. She'd been making it up. But mud sticks.

I'm here to see him. The waiting room is full of uncomfortable people on uncomfortable sofas. They sit in silence. Their children ask questions like, 'How much longer, Mum?', and 'What's wrong with you, anyway?', but they never get an answer, just a dirty look or a slap on the leg. The sofas line the edge of the room like a skirting board. There's a coffee table covered with women's magazines, three beer mats jammed under one of the legs. The only time anyone moves is when a name gets called. There's usually a pause. Then someone stands up. All heads turn and look at the person daring to be next in the queue, sneer until they reach the door-to-the-corridor-that-leads-to-the-doctor. Because they dared to get called in before them.

I sit as close to the door as possible.

'Steven Johnson, please.'

There's the pause. A young woman holds her hand out to the boy sitting next to her. He's got slug-like snot trails up his sleeves and a shaved head, which means he's more than likely had nits. He grabs her hand and she drags him across the room. His feet barely touch the ground. She opens the door, puts her palm on the back of his bald head and shoves him into the corridor.

'Hello Mrs Johnson. Hello Steven. Come in. Sit down.'

He's left the intercom on.

'How can I help?'

Turn the intercom off. Please turn the intercom off.

'It's him. He's still pissing his pants. He's making my life a misery.'

The waiting room moves. The young couple in the corner shuffle closer together. They hold hands and look at the floor. A man in his seventies picks up a copy of

Vogue and starts flicking through the pages. A woman starts coughing. Then someone else starts coughing. Now we're all coughing. But it makes no difference, we can hear everything.

'It's not uncommon for a child of Steven's age to have this problem. Have you spoken to him about it? Is there anything bothering him at school? It could be stress.'

'He's eight-years-old.'

'That doesn't matter. If he's worried about something, he could still be suffering from stress. That could be why he's wetting himself.'

There it is again. Only a politer version. The waiting room shakes. Smiles crack all over. These people are supposed to be ill.

'Steven, is there anything you want to talk about? Are you having problems at school?'

'No.'

'Do you like school?'

'No.'

'Do you have any nice friends there?'

'No.'

'Are you a good boy for your mum?'

'Yes.'

'Mrs Johnson?'

'He's a little bastard.'

'I think Steven is suffering from stress. I think that you should go into school and have a word with the teachers. In the meantime, there's something we can do to help.'

'He'll take anything.'

'We can provide him with special under-wear.'

There's a shuffling of papers, an opening of drawers, a sound like a telephone struggling to connect. Then there is silence.

'Do you think he knows he left it on?' says the woman next to me. But I don't answer because Angelica is backing into the door and pushing it open with her high heel, shaking her umbrella. She's wearing a long black coat with fluffy cuffs. She has her hood up. Now she's talking to the girl on reception. She's taking her hood down. It's definitely Angelica.

'Gordon Kingdom, please,' says the voice over the intercom. She's asking the girl something, but I can't hear what she's saying. I think they're arguing. Or Angelica's arguing. The girl is smiling. The moment Angelica turns her back, the girl will spin round to the nurse flicking through files behind her. She'll mouth the word 'bitch', or something worse.

'Gordon Kingdom, please. Gordon Kingdom.'

I stand up, get ready for the sneers. But Mrs Johnson drags Steven back into the waiting room and everyone looks at him instead. She's got him by the wrists. There's a bulge around his waistline. It looks like he's wearing a rubber ring beneath his tiny trousers.

'Is that thing turned off?'

'What thing?'

'The intercom.'

'Of course it is. Come in, sit down.'

'Let me get my coat off.'

'So how are we?'

'We're fine.'

'Good to hear. How can I help? Just the prescription?'

'No. I'd like everything checked.'

'Gordon, I checked everything last time. Everything looks fine. I want to know how you're feeling in general. I want to know how you're coping. Are you still writing things down?'

'All that stopped. That's fine now. I feel fine.'

'You're not forgetful?'

'I make a few notes.'

'That's good.'

'But I'm sure I get headaches.'

'We've been over this before. It's the stress. It's inevitable.'

'I want everything checked.'

'There's no point, Gordon. It's a waste of time. For both of us.'

'I want everything checked.'

★ ★ ★

Doctor Morris has a notice board stuck to the wall behind his desk. I stare at it while he pokes and prods me. It's covered in leaflets and information booklets. A mixture of colours and slogans. Do this. Eat that. Say no. Don't be caught without one. 0% interest free credit. Buy one, get one free. There are six anti-smoking posters. They make me want a cigarette and I don't even smoke. They're for the drivers. The men in lorries, dozers, bowsers and dumpers. The 120s, the D8s and the Triple 7s. This is a town surrounded by coal and men in their machines. Eleven hours a day. Always smoking. One after another. A constant flow of toxins sucked inside. Men barely talking out the sides of their mouths. Men who have no need to talk. Always alone, in a cabin full of smoke and dust.

It was in the paper. One of the lorries, headfirst off the face of the cut. The driver hung over the steering wheel, his lifeless face pressed against the windscreen. The yellow hairs in his moustache, splayed all over. Pictures of a 200 loading shovel picking up the broken lorry, like a metal parent. It was summer. The driver's bare chest ripped open by the fall. His black lungs coated with earth and glass, layer upon layer of dirt. His grey heart giving up. Submitting. A group of men dragging him from his cab, laying him on the floor, standing over him with their hands on their hips. Their machines still humming where they left them. A mixture of half-grief and silence. From the sides of their mouths.

They're supposed to read these posters and care.

★ ★ ★

'There's nothing wrong with you, Gordon.'

'Have you checked?'

'Yes, I've checked. You know I've checked. I always check. There's still nothing wrong with you.'

'Okay.'

'Let me sign your prescription.'

'What about the headaches?'

'Maybe you should try to get more sleep. Drink plenty of water.'

'I drink tea. And I've started baking.'

'That's fine. Drinking tea is fine. Try drinking water as well. You'd be surprised what difference a glass of water can make. What do you bake?'

'I don't really drink water.'

'Well now would be a good time to start.'

'Sometimes it comes out brown. I bake cakes.'

'You can always buy water from the supermarket or the shop. They sell it everywhere.'

'Water?'

'It's good for you.'

'I'm not paying for water.'

'That's up to you. Here's Georgina's prescription. How is she?'

'She's fine.'

'I should really see her soon. It would be nice to meet her, check her over.'

'I don't think that will be necessary.'

'Well I'm glad she's doing well, but you should still make her an appointment.' Doctor Morris hands me the prescription. He stands up, walks to the door and opens it. I should follow him, but something stops me. I stay seated, my back to him, staring at the colours and slogans. 'Gordon?' he says, closing the door again. Doctor Morris returns to his desk, stands at my side and puts his hand on my shoulder. I want to put my hand on his, but I don't. He's not here for comfort.

'What if it happens to me?' I say. He pauses for one, two, three seconds. Then he shakes my shoulder and removes his hand. He walks back to the door and turns the handle.

'Gordon, you're absolutely fine. Just get some rest and look after yourself. You know where I am if anything happens.'

'Thank you, Doctor. I trust your judgement.'

'No problem. No problem at all.'

'You did nothing wrong.'

'Sorry?'

'That girl.'

'Right. I know that, Gordon.'

★ ★ ★

Angelica is still arguing with the receptionist. There's no sign of Mrs Johnson or her son. I wonder if he's on his way home or being dragged round shops, his new underpants full to the brim, urine sloshing round the tops of his legs. I stand behind Angelica, hold my breath so she can't feel it on her neck. That's how close I am. She has her hair in a ponytail and a spot beneath her hairline. It looks ripe for squeezing. I could squeeze it.

'Olivia Sergeant, please.'

An elderly woman struggles to stand up. She holds her walking stick at an angle and tries to force herself upright. What little weight she has relies upon that stick. I picture a child running up and kicking it from under her, bored with waiting for her bones to work. I imagine the old woman's withered frame tumbling to the floor like a vase to concrete. She starts making her way across the room

towards the door-to-the-corridor-that-leads-
to-the-doctors. Her feet make tiny steps. Her
hands shake. No-one goes to help her.
No-one says, 'Would you like a hand?' or, 'Let
me take your bags for you'. Everyone sits and
stares. Just a roomful of eyes.

'Olivia Sergeant, please. Olivia Sergeant.'

I turn my head and take a deep breath
while no-one is watching. I hold it for as long
as possible. Angelica smells of perfume and
cigarettes. Someone else's habit in my
nostrils. I imagine feeling young again. Then I
breathe out. I wonder if she felt it. I wonder if
she can smell the breakfast on my breath. I
think about sitting in the kitchen, waiting for
the toaster to pop. Breakfast with Angelica.

'When are you going to fix that toaster?'
she says.

'There's nothing wrong with the toaster.'

'It sparks blue when you put the toast in.'

'You don't put toast in the toaster. You put
bread in the toaster.'

'Don't be clever. It needs fixing.'

'I'll do it at the weekend.'

She comes and sits on my knee. Her
dressing gown presses against my skin. She
puts her arm round my neck and her hand
through my hair. She spills crumbs down us
both, then brushes them off with my tie. We
sit at the table. I hold her close. Bounce her

up and down like a baby. She laughs, and every time she bounces it jars her belly. So she laughs even harder. We laugh together. Then I kiss her goodbye and leave for work.

'Keep your fucking prescription,' she says. 'And by the way, you've got lipstick on your teeth.'

The girl behind reception sits in silence and smiles sweetly as Angelica flicks her ponytail and marches out the door, straight past me. She watches through the window, holds out her arm and raises her middle finger. Then she rubs her teeth with it. I keep watching Angelica as she walks across the car park. She stumbles and bends down to put her shoe back into place. A man walks round the corner. He's wearing a suit and carrying a briefcase. Angelica stands up quickly. They stop, exchange glares, say nothing. The man walks away to wherever he's going. Angelica stands on the tarmac. White lines all around her. Boxes for cars just waiting for owners, like dogs tied to lampposts.

Disguise

I'm standing in front of the mirror in the bedroom. Georgina is lying on the bed behind me. Her pillows are plumped and her face is pale. She is dead to the world. I'm wearing a balaclava and staring at myself through the tiny holes where my eyes fit. I'm wearing black shoes, black trousers, and a black jumper underneath a black coat. Black fingerless gloves. I look like someone about to reconstruct a burglary for the television, not a man in his fifties. I shake the ends of my fingers and move my neck from side to side. I bend down to stretch my hamstrings. Then I stand again, take up some kind of boxing stance, throw a few jabs. Come on Gordon, I say to myself. Come on old timer, you can do it. Ten minutes and it'll all be over. No-one will notice. If they do, they'll probably thank you. You'll get cards through the letterbox. Nice one Gordon, they'll say. You did the right thing. I take a deep breath and blink a few times. I walk downstairs, open the front door and step outside.

It's half past four in the morning. Benny's light went out two hours ago. There are

40

clouds in the sky, dark grey and navy. They sit like a child sits at the top of the stairs, listening to parents arguing. Aware of everything. I hear a crack, a nothing sound. It's absolutely nothing. Pull yourself together. Then again, think of the logic. Someone will always notice. No they won't. There's no-one around. I walk slowly across the street with my knees bent, as quietly as possible. I hold my arms out to the sides, palms flat for balance. It's a new walk. If I saw someone doing this, I'd file it under 'Suspicious behaviour'.

★ ★ ★

Now I'm in Don Donald's back garden. I climbed over the fence and landed in his compost heap, which is mostly made up of decaying food. There's a stray sausage on the lawn. It must have rolled off, or he's left it there on purpose for the birds. Frost is forming on the grass. It's beginning to go hard and crunches under my feet as I walk carefully to the shed. I open the door and step inside, closing it behind me.

There's a window with a crack in it. The moonlight shines through and illuminates the wooden walls. I look around me. I've not been in here for years. A dartboard hangs on the back of the door. It has two pictures on it. The Queen Mother pinned to the double top. And a blonde girl in her twenties. She has sweet blue eyes and a dart through her forehead. There's a wooden desk under the window. It has nails, screws, nuts, bolts, drill bits and pornography on it. A magazine opened at the centre. Black, finger-shaped grease marks smeared along the edges. There's a puddle on the floor and a hole in the roof. The wood is rotting and coated with moss. Along the wall is a line of nails. Some have tools hanging from them, others just shapes of tools drawn round with a felt tip pen. There's a hammer where a spanner should be. Useless nails holding imaginary pliers. In one corner of the shed, there's a lawn mower. An old petrol mower from the 1970s. It looks like a tank. And in another corner a bucket, full to the brim with scrunched up balls of tissue paper. There's one on the floor next to my foot. I try to kick it towards the bin but it sticks to the floor. I open drawers. Start looking for my hedge trimmers.

★ ★ ★

There's a tree opposite my house, on the other side of the road. It's the smallest tree on the street. It was planted by a group of children as part of a school project. They came marching down the road, holding hands and pulling faces. The mayor came and posed for pictures. It seems that's all she ever does. Hangs chains around her neck and grins. Her teeth shining like she's got a torch in her mouth. They stood in a circle round the tree. The mayor, the children, and a man from the council. He did the planting. I remember his face, all out of shape, trying to smile.

The tree's now ten feet high with just a handful of branches and even fewer leaves. It looks like a short telegraph pole. When people talk about the trees on Cressington Vale, they always count seven. They forget about the withered post planted by the children to celebrate Diwali. It's a nuisance. They fractured the pipes when they dug the hole. That's why the water's brown. When the tree loses what leaves it has, they land in the drain directly below. They block it so that when it rains, the street floods. Last year, it rained so hard the water ran into gardens and ruined lawns. It has a plaque nailed into its trunk. The Joanne Gaubert memorial tree. No-one knows who she was. She could be anyone. She might not even be dead.

The tree stands outside Angelica's house.

I can't see her television.

Note: Phase 1 = find trimmers. Phase 2 = remove branches. Phase 3 = dispose of branches. Phase 4 = remove trunk. Phase 5 = dispose of trunk. Risk factor = 9.5. Note end.

I'm by the tree. My balaclava keeps slipping and it's making my face hot. I can feel myself sweating. I found the hedge trimmers under a pile of old newspapers. I knew he had them. I was right. Don Donald has become a liar. I give the trimmers a test. A giant pair of scissors. He's looked after them well. He's sharpened them and put new handles on. I try a few snips in mid air. They sound good. Efficient. I start on the branches. They come off easily. I do them one at a time and pile them up on the pavement. When I've finished, I take them to the skip outside John Bonsall's house. He's having a conservatory put in. I saw the van pull up this morning. The skip is barely half full, just soil and stone. And a bicycle wheel. I throw the branches on top and walk back to the tree. A bare trunk. I pull my sleeve up and look at my watch. I've been outside an hour. I can hear the hedgerows rustling. Soon the birds will start to twitter. It used to wake me up before I went to work. Before they put the double glazing in.

I open the hedge trimmers as far as they'll

go and hold them where the two blades cross. The metal is freezing. I can feel it through my gloves, the cold working its way through my fingers. I need to be quick before they stiffen up. I twist my shoulders, flex my arms and start hacking at the trunk of the tree. It jars my shoulders and sends a pain up my back and neck. But I keep going, keep gripping the metal and slashing away at the tree. My wrists begin to ache, so I try using the weight from my hips to turn and hack. Turn and hack. It's working. I'm half an inch in. I stop a second to catch my breath. I look up at the houses. Benny is standing at his bedroom window with the light switched off. I recognise his silhouette. I've no idea if he can see me. I stand perfectly still and wait for him to disappear. It takes almost three minutes.

I look at the tiny indent in the side of the tree. The fruits of my labour. The sky is losing darkness. Not much, only ever so slightly, but I know it's happening. I can make out the colour of things. Reflections in house windows. The yellow skip with patches of rust on it. Parked cars, two lines of deep maroon. Angelica's big blue door with the peeling paint. Even my clothes are getting lighter. They look less black. I hear a noise in the distance. A whirring sound, like the draught through a gap in a door. Bottles, close enough to shake in the wind, vibrate against each other. I can hear them rattling. Someone whistling. The milkman.

I close the hedge trimmers and hurry towards the house. I arch my back and lift my head. Another new walk. This one to make me look guiltless. But that's impossible. I'm wearing a balaclava. So I walk quicker, through the gate and into the garden. I jog the last few steps to the door, struggle with the key and barge inside. I climb upstairs to the spare room and watch the milk float trundle along. It crawls past the half-ruined tree and the skip full of branches. I can see the colour in the milkman's cheeks. They're red from the cold. His lips pursed with whistling.

I look at Angelica's window. The curtains drawn. The flowers on the sill.

The branches are gone.

It's better than nothing.

Escalation

Georgina has had her second stroke in eighteen months. It happened on New Years Day. The day before Angelica moved in and the day before my birthday. Angelica's birthday. We'd spent the afternoon in the garden with our coats on. She wore the mittens I'd bought her, even put them on herself. It was bitterly cold, but we didn't mind. Georgina didn't mind. Kipling sat on her lap while I planted the Christmas tree. Don Donald came across in his pyjamas. He said he'd run out of pickled onions and would I make him up a new jar. Then Georgina stood up, walked to the wall of the house and around the garden. She used the fence to keep her balance. I almost cried.

Hours later, I found her on the bed, her towel on the floor by the dresser. She'd just had a bath on her own. I'd dried her hair and she'd dried her legs. Then I'd left the room to get her a glass of water so she could take her tablets. It had been a long day. I'd expected her to fall asleep while I was downstairs. I thought I'd have to shake her shoulder to wake her up. But when I got back, she wasn't asleep. She was still in position, pillows plumped as always. Just how they needed to be. She was awake. Her eyes glazed over, her mouth disfigured. One side lower than it should have been. Perfectly still. Perfectly calm.

I sat with her for a while. Less than a minute. Then I walked back downstairs to the kitchen, opened the cupboard under the sink and took out my manual. There were no tears. No ambulances. No-one saw it happen. She'd been getting better.

★　★　★

'Why don't you try writing things down, Gordon? It might help you remember.'

'What am I supposed to write?'

'Anything and everything. Just jot down what you need to. Get yourself a notebook you can put in your pocket. If there's something you need to remember, you can write it down. You'll always have it. Structure, Gordon. You need structure.'

'Okay. I'll think about it.'

'Well make sure you do. Let me write that prescription.'

★　★　★

I went straight to Wilkinson and bought a children's notebook. It was all they had left. It was pink with a cartoon bumblebee in the top right hand corner. I put my thumb in its face each time I opened the book. The first thing I wrote was a shopping list. I can still remember it. Milk, bread and a tub of wet wipes. Then on the way home, I ran into Mick Batty. I used to work with him. He stopped me and asked me how Georgina was getting on. I said she was doing fine. I told him she was talking properly again and that they thought she'd make a full recovery. He told me nothing had changed in the office. My desk was still empty. I wasn't worth replacing. He laughed when he said it. And I laughed with him. Then he told me he'd married an 'Oriental piece from down south'. I asked him what her name was. He said he couldn't pronounce it, so he usually called her Roy, 'Because that's what it sounds like'. When I got home, I opened my notebook and transcribed our conversation. I wrote 'Roy?' in the margin. Underlined the question mark.

Over time, my notes gave me structure, purpose and something to do. Like I had before the stroke. Like I was told I needed. They took my mind off Georgina. They kept me sane. I made lists of my clothes. Colours, materials and sizes. Underpants and over-coats. And I set myself challenges. I went to the mini-market, wrote down the names of all the checkout staff. I went there every day, even if I didn't want to buy anything. The aim was to collect a full seven days' rota. Charlotte, Christopher, Donna, Emily, Hannah, Katy and Lisi with an 's'. I can remember them all. Not one from M to Z. I made alphabetised lists of items in the house. Books in order. Records in order. Compact discs in order. Even though we only had five of them. Then I began to write down what I'd done each day. Where I'd been. Who I'd spoken to. I joined the library, but never borrowed books. I'd go in and pretend to read. I'd sit at the table with my back to the librarian, my notepad hidden under my arm. There were thirty-three cookery books in the food and drink section. I copied out every single recipe in full. But I never stayed there long. I had to get back to Georgina. It took me ten hours over sixteen days. Nine pads of A4.

★　★　★

Then I saw the Jehovah's Witness' mistress.

I began watching the street from the

50

window. I made notes on my neighbours, studied their routines, learnt to predict their behaviour. Lights switched off. Cars in drives. Children meeting curfews. I stored my notebooks in the loft and bought some files from Wilkinson. Twenty-six sliding folders and a hundred A4 pads. They supplied a van to drive them to the house. The driver said, 'What the hell are you going to do with this lot?' and I said, 'I'm going to build a bookcase.' And I did. I bought plywood from B&Q and built a bookcase in the spare room. I labelled the files from A to Z. Then I stuck sixteen pieces of paper together and pencilled out a map of the street. I drew round a coaster, made squares for houses. Outside each square, I pressed firmly with a felt tip pen to make a dot, a different colour for every neighbour. Rectangles for cars and trees made from netting, stuck to the map with Pritt Stick. I found an old picture of Kipling and drawing-pinned him to the front garden. When I'd finished, I hung it on the wall. I wrote 'Cressington Vale' in the bottom right hand corner. My system was in place.

★ ★ ★

And then I saw Benny painting.

I watched him close his eyes and stroke the

51

canvas with his brush. I was mesmerised. He was different from the rest. Don Donald with his hands in his pockets, Andrea with her towel and Ina in her chair. They are ordinary people with ordinary lives. But Benny isn't ordinary. Benny paints pictures with his eyes closed. I don't know why he does what he does. I don't know what happens when he closes his eyes. I don't know what his pictures look like. Watching Benny feels like being somewhere else. It feels like something out of the ordinary is happening. It feels like I am part of a secret. I stop writing notes and I think about God. I ask him to save me. I ask him to save Georgina. This is the time I keep for myself. Last thing at night. First hours of morning.

But now Angelica is here. Her file is thick already. She doesn't go to work, but she gets up early. There's been no visit from a husband and there's no sign of children. She is friendly, but she isn't my friend. I don't know what she is. I speak to her as often as possible, but sometimes I don't know what to say. Her door is now pink. And orange. And green. It reminds me of her toenails. She painted it last weekend. I watched her walking in and out of the house. Coffee breaks, cigarette breaks and television breaks. It took her six hours. All the light in the day.

I had to start a new file.

'Why don't you try writing things down, Gordon? It might help you remember. We know it's not been easy for you.'

So I did, and now it is. I never miss a trick. Life is easier because I have my files.

★   ★   ★

This morning, like every morning, I woke at six. I walked from the spare room downstairs to the kitchen and made myself breakfast. I ate at the table. Kipling was asleep in his basket. I watched his ribcage rise and fall with his breathing, so slowly and with such long pauses in between that twice I stopped eating and waited for his next breath, made sure he hadn't died. I finished my breakfast, put my plate in the sink and opened the cupboard underneath. I took out my manual: How to help your wife recover from a stroke in little under eighteen months, by Gordon Kingdom. It has everything in it. Everything we need. It's thicker than my bible.

I wrote it all down. Every single detail.

The appointments, the tablets, the positions, the procedures. The do's, the what definitely not to do's and the what to do as a last resorts. The endless calculations. The graphs in rough and the graphs on graph paper. The facts, the figures and the mimicking of specialists. The doctors, the nurses and the physiotherapists. The speech therapists and the pain managers with the impossible job. Her incredible pain. Our incredible pain. It's all in the manual. We did it all by the book.

And she got better.

We were getting better.

Extractions

We grew up together but went to different schools. I lived on one side of the void, she lived on the other. The void was Gutterton Half, a 150-foot deep opencast pit in the shape of a semi-circle. At its widest it stretched 100 yards, at its longest 200 yards. It was the town's first coal extraction. They created a wall of soil around the site to block the sound. Vast heaps of freshly-seeded grass to hide an abyss of clay and coal. They've been tearing it out the ground ever since.

My father worked with Georgina's father at Gutterton Half. Everyone's father worked at Gutterton Half. Mine was a lorry driver, hers worked a loading shovel. One picked the coal up, the other drove it away. They worked twelve hours a day, from seven in the morning until seven at night. When they loaded the lorry, they communicated with hand signals, nods and winks. When they weren't loading the lorry, one of them drove and one of them waited. Both smoking in silence. They only spoke during half-hour lunch breaks. Enough to strike a friendship. We used to alternate Sunday lunch between the two houses. Two families sat together eating properly round a table. Our parents, Georgina and me. Her father swore constantly. Almost every other word. He slid obscenities into sentences where you least expected them — 'Mary woman, get-yerself-to-fucking-gether' — and after a while, you hardly noticed because he made it sound so normal. My father was a man of the church. He never swore once. Not that I heard.

After lunch, our parents moved to the comfy chairs and drank until they were drunk. Our fathers drank whiskey, our mothers drank gin. We were thirteen-years-old and took it in turns to escort them home. It was our job. While they were drinking we'd have to occupy ourselves because they wanted us out of the house. Mostly, we didn't speak. We had nothing in common. I was a boy, she was a girl. What was there to talk about? So we'd end up walking through the woods to the park behind Georgina's school, where there were always other children. Sometimes, she'd speak to them and I'd have to stand next to her and wait. She looked much older than me. They asked if I was her younger brother. But I didn't mind. It was better than standing on my own.

One day, instead of going to the park, Georgina decided we would walk out to the void. We climbed through a hole in the fence and sat on one of the huge soil heaps looking down into the pit. It was the middle of summer and the air was shimmering in the heat. We could see the machines lined up stationary for the weekend. They looked tiny, like toys. We were there for over an hour. And we began to talk. I told her I was sick of my father telling me what to do all the time. I said I never understood how he could go to church in the morning and then drink all afternoon. I said it didn't seem right. Georgina told me she thought her mother wanted to kill herself. Then she kissed me.

★ ★ ★

Georgina was my girlfriend between the ages of thirteen and almost sixteen, even though we only saw each other on Sundays. She later said she never told her friends about us, whereas I'd told anyone willing to listen. We carried on as we always had, except we talked more, and we kissed each other when we ran out of things to say. She used to tell me the things she'd overheard her mother saying to herself in the bathroom. I found it hard to make her feel better. I tried, but my heart wasn't in it. I was just pleased to be there. It was fantastic.

When she turned sixteen, just five weeks before I did, Georgina decided to stop being my girlfriend. She took me back to the soil heap at Gutterton Half and told me it was time we both grew up. We needed to spend more time with friends from our own schools. I agreed with her, walked home alone and put my head under my pillow. Unfortunately, our parents still had Sunday lunch together, and we still had the job of making sure they got home. But Georgina soon resigned her post, she disappeared completely. When we went to their house, she was always out. When they came to our house, her parents phoned for a taxi.

It was three years before I saw her again, at her father's funeral. He'd been taken to hospital with flu, or as my mother put it, 'just a cold'. The following day he got pneumonia. The day after that he died. It happened so quickly that they decided to open him up. His lungs were riddled with cancer and had been for years. He'd never told a soul. My father was devastated. He stood with Georgina's mother as they lowered the coffin into the ground. I had to stand with a crowd of relatives and half-friends, listening to the whispers. 'He used to knock her about, you know,' and 'When's the buffet starting?'

Family members were invited to throw

earth into the grave. When Georgina's turn came, she declined. She kept her hands clasped behind her back, her eyes fixed on the ground. Even when they asked her a second time, she didn't reply. I watched her throughout the ceremony. She looked the same as she had when I saw her last: tall, slim and anxious. It made me realise how much I'd changed myself. I had shorter hair, cut by a barber instead of my mother. And I wore clothes that fit me. If I wanted, I could almost grow a moustache.

I decided to speak to her. The wake was held at the community centre, which backed out onto the park we used to walk to together. I waited until the buffet had cleared and she was on her own. I watched her go through the fire exit at the back of the room. She sat on a swing with her plate on her lap and a plastic cup jammed between her knees. The cup was filled with cheap, sparkling wine. Everyone had to have one. Her mother insisted. The mood had turned from sadness to celebration. Smiles and laughter. Though no-one said, 'It's what he would have wanted.'

I picked up my cup, downed my drink and followed Georgina through the fire exit. She smiled as I approached her. I could smell her perfume. She'd started wearing it just weeks before we split up. It seemed stronger than I remembered. I sat on the swing next to hers. I wanted to say something useful, something profound. We hadn't seen each other for so long. But I turned towards her, opened my mouth and said nothing. I had absolutely nothing to say to her. And after a few seconds of silence, we laughed.

'So, my mother's not killed herself yet.'

'I noticed.'

'I don't think she ever will.'

'No? Well, that's good news.'

'I'll have to put her in a home instead.'

We'd been outside an hour when the disco started. Someone turned all the lights off apart from the one by the bar. We heard a loud cheer. I could see my parents dancing in the doorway by the entrance. Twisting and shouting. And Mary, Georgina's mother. One arm in the air, the other round the DJ. Her hips all over.

No-one came to look for us.

First strike

Nearly forty years later, almost eighteen months ago, Georgina had her first stroke. I'd arranged a neighbourhood watch meeting. Seven of us sat round a table in the Shoulder of Mutton. It was bank holiday weekend and the pub was full of people. I sat at the head of the table. On my left, Andrea Turner, John Bonsall and Georgina. On my right, Peter and Janice Smith, then Don Donald. Ina Macaukey's morning milk had been stolen five times in two weeks. We had important things to discuss.

'It's just milk, Gordon.'

'Janice, it might just be milk to you, but it's not just milk to me and it's not just milk to Ina. Remember, you might be next.'

'Maybe it's the milkman.'

'I don't think the milkman would need to steal someone else's milk,' said John. 'He probably gets it free.'

'He's got something wrong about him.'

'Everyone's got something wrong about them,' said Peter. 'And anyway, why would he keep taking it from the same person? No-one's that stupid.'

'Here we go, straight away. My husband thinks I'm stupid.'

'It's not the milkman,' I interrupted. 'I asked him yesterday. He explained himself and said he knows nothing. And I believe him. We've obviously not been watching well enough. One of us should have noticed something unusual.'

'Ina can have some of our milk, Gordon,' said John. 'We always get an extra bottle.'

'No, that's not the point.'

'It wouldn't cause a problem. It's just milk.'

'Stop saying that. It's never just milk. Theft is theft.'

I shuffled my papers and tapped the end of my biro on the table. Blank faces stared back at me. I glared at Don. He nodded.

'Gordon is kind of right, everyone. At the moment it's just milk, but that could lead to something more serious.'

'Like what?' said Peter.

'I don't know. Cars? One thing leads to another.'

'That's ridiculous.'

'It's not ridiculous,' I said. 'It's exactly why we need to take this matter seriously and exactly why we need to work out a shift pattern. We can do that this evening. Don's kindly brought some graph paper and I've got a packet of felt tips.'

'What do you mean by shift pattern?' said Andrea.

'So we can keep watch.'

'I object to that.'

'No objections. We need to work out who's going to keep watch and when. The best way is to take shifts. So far, the milk's been stolen at least once every three days and always between the time it arrives and the time we wake up. If we do our jobs properly, we'll have our thief in no time. We can begin tomorrow.'

'I'll take five until six tomorrow morning,' said Don.

'Thank you. That leaves four until five and six until seven. Andrea, which would you like?'

'I can't object?'

'No, you can't object. Which shift would you like?'

'It's bank holiday. Why don't we start all this next week?'

'Right, I'll put you down for the early shift tomorrow.'

'No. Six until seven. I'll do six until seven.'

'Thank you, Andrea.'

'We'll do the same shift the day after,' said Janice.

'Will we?' said Peter.

'Yes, you will.'

'Gordon?'

'Yes, John?' I said.

'Would you mind if Pamela and I went to see my mother? We were planning to drive up tomorrow and stay there the night, you see. Will that affect the schedule?'

'So, you're away from the street on Monday, but you're here tomorrow morning. How does four until five sound?'

'Well, that does make it rather a long day. She lives in Glasgow. Could I perhaps do two hours instead of one when we get back?'

'Well, maybe Andrea could swap her shift with you.'

'Objection,' said Andrea.

'Then I'm afraid it's going to have to be tomorrow. No-one can do two consecutive shifts. It's just not practical. It'll give you more time to pack.'

'What if we don't want to take part in this nonsense?' said Peter.

'Then someone will steal your milk.'

Don raised his hand, 'Gordon, when are you keeping watch?'

'I don't mind. Of course, one of you may find our thief in the morning. If not, we could do our shift the day after. Georgina, what do you think? We could walk Kipling early and be back for seven?'

The moment is framed as a painting on a

nail in my mind. Our table, six heads all turned towards my wife. Behind them a room full of people. Moving, talking and drinking. And then Georgina, perfectly still in her chair. Her head cocked slightly to the left, her face lopsided. Her arms lifeless in her lap. A man wearing pleated trousers passed behind her. I remember they were pinstriped. He spilt some of his drink and brushed the back of her chair. But she didn't notice. She was busy somewhere else. Somewhere new. And I remember her eyes. Wild and detached. Searching a whole new world. The old one lost forever.

$\star$ $\star$ $\star$

Don Donald was the first to react. He ran round the table and wrapped his coat around Georgina's shoulders. Andrea shouted, 'Can you hear me? Georgina, can you hear what I'm saying?' and Peter rushed to the bar to get the landlord to ring for an ambulance. Janice followed him, but the job was done by the time she got there. John Bonsall started crying. He sat next to me. I could feel him shaking. Within seconds a small crowd had gathered, but Don stood up and asked them all to go away. 'Please, I have everything under control,' he said.

And I just sat there. I said nothing. I did nothing. I watched the paramedics arrive and lift my wife into a wheelchair. They checked her pulse and spoke to her. They told her exactly what they were doing. Behind them, people continued with their talking and their drinking. They turned around every so often to look at the table with the paralysed woman and the man in tears. 'Oh, that's awful,' they said. 'Such a tragedy.' Don asked Andrea to take John outside. Peter and Janice were already there. Everyone had their role. They'd been to flag down the ambulance. Don waved his hand in front of my face and said, 'Gordon, they're taking her now. You should go with her.'

'Are you going?'

'I can if you want me too.'

'That would be nice.'

'Give me your car keys. I'll follow the ambulance.'

The hospital waiting room was full of people like me. Dumbstruck husbands, wives and lovers. And people like Don, there to provide the transport home. We sat together on cheap plastic seats, drank tea and waited for updates. I listened to the women on reception. The way they switched their conversations and changed their tone of voice. Soft and understanding with the in-patients. Laughs and jokes with each other. Don tried to speak to me, attempted conversation. He put his hand on my shoulder. 'She'll be okay,' he kept saying. 'They'll have her right in no time.' And I didn't mind him saying it, even though I knew it wasn't true.

Eventually, a doctor came to speak to us. He was tall and under thirty. His spectacles hung from a chain around his neck. He told us he was sorry about the wait. He said Georgina was stable but sleeping, and that I could see her if I wanted. I followed him down a long corridor and into a tiny room. They'd moved her to a bed and hooked her up to wires, tubes and machines, like an extra in a film or one of the people wheeled past us in the waiting room. She didn't look like my wife. I turned around and walked away. The doctor followed me.

'Mr Kingdom, are you all right?'

'Fine, thank you.' He was chasing me down the corridor. I tried to speed up.

'You're wife's going to need to stay here tonight. Have you got any clothes for her?'

'Don picked them up. He gave them to the nurse. I'll come and get her tomorrow.'

'She may be here a little longer than that, I'm afraid. She won't be able to leave tomorrow. She's had a very serious stroke.' I

was back in the waiting room. I grabbed Don
by the arm and ushered him out the door.

'Mr Kingdom?'

'I think they're calling you, Gordon.'

'It's fine, everything's going to be fine. Like
you said.'

I got in the car and started the engine. Don
climbed in beside me. I pulled out the car
park, looked in the rear view mirror. The
doctor and the receptionist were stood in the
entrance waving their arms. The automatic
doors opened and closed behind them. I kept
driving. Don sat fidgeting nervously in the
passenger seat. After a few minutes silence, I
pulled into Cressington Vale. It was half past
midnight. I parked up and undid my seatbelt.
Don did the same. I continued to say
nothing. I sat, and I stared.

'So, what happened? I mean, she must be
okay. You spoke to her, I take it?'

'I wasn't able to speak to her.'

'They wouldn't let you speak to her?'

'She was sleeping.'

'Well, that's understandable. How long will
she be in for?'

'They didn't say. It could take a while.'

'Would you like me to go with you in the
morning?'

'I'll ring the hospital first.'

'You know, Gordon, if there's anything I

can do, you just need to ask. She's going to need some looking after when she gets home.'

'They'll send someone out, I expect.'

'Yes, but anything you need. I'm only over the road.'

'Thank you, Don.'

He nodded at me and smiled with his mouth closed. It was a helpless smile. I pressed the button on the dashboard that unlocks the doors. He stepped out of the car and into the street. He kicked his heels on the kerb, tapped his fingers on the bonnet. I wanted to say thank you.

'Don,' I said.

'Yes, Gordon?'

'Don't forget your shift in the morning.'

God almighty

It's easier to watch Angelica from behind a curtain than it is to go unnoticed when you're following her down the street. It's now twenty-four minutes past nine and I'm on my way to church. Angelica has lived on Cressington Vale for almost a fortnight. Each morning, she leaves the house between nine and half past. She returns with three newspapers, which are never the same, although at least one of them will have a free CD attached or a picture of a naked woman on the cover. The newsagent is on the main road, fifty yards from the corner of Cressington Vale. Angelica has dropped her bag and is crouched on the floor, picking up her belongings. She's wearing the same black fluffy-cuffed coat she wears when she goes to the doctors, winter gloves and a pair of pink slippers with nothing covering her toes. The slippers must be new, her hands must be warm and her feet must be freezing. I can see this from my position, also crouched on the floor, twenty yards behind, on the opposite side of the road, under a hedge.

'Gordon, are you all right down there?'

John Bonsall is towering above me. I stand up quickly and scratch my forehead on a branch. He's on his way to B&Q. He goes every Sunday to buy food for his plants. The smallest packet available. So it's always fresh.

'Have you lost something?'

'I thought I saw a hedgehog.'

'Really?'

'But I didn't.'

'What was it?'

'I don't know.'

'You've been down there an awfully long time.'

'Yes. You're right.'

'We have a hedgehog that comes into our back garden. Pamela likes to leave a saucer of milk by the gnome. It's always gone in the morning. The milk, not the saucer. Or the gnome. Sometimes she leaves food as well. He rather enjoys the odd biscuit. We call him Harry. Harry the hedgehog. Pamela said it had to have a name. I wasn't so sure, what with the kids and everything. We don't want them coming home from school to find poor Harry's been hit by a car. Squished and squashed.'

I'm barely listening. Angelica has gathered her items and put them back in her bag. She walks away from us and into the newsagent. Mass starts in fifteen minutes. I'm getting later.

71

'When's that skip going to be moved, John?'

'Someone's filled it full of branches. I think it was the same person who vandalised the memorial tree. Pamela said she heard someone in the street the night it happened.'

'Probably a drunk.'

'I rang the police.'

'The police?'

'Yes, of course.'

'What for?'

'I told them I was innocent.'

'What did they say?'

'Not much. They've not even been out to look at it. It's only a tree, apparently. Try telling that to the children at Diwali.'

'I really should be going.'

'How are you anyway, Gordon? How's Georgina? We've not seen her since Christmas. Is she still doing well?'

'We're both fine. I'm sorry John, I do need to go or I'll be late for church.'

I try to get away, but Angelica has left the newsagent and is walking back towards us. She's carrying her newspapers. One has breasts on the front. Two have CDs. I'll write it down when I get home. She's reading the back of one of the papers. Now she's looking up and across at us. I think she's smiling.

'Do you know that lady, Gordon?'

'Yes, I do.'

'Who is she?'

'She's called Angelica.'

'Like the plant?'

'What plant?'

'Angelica is a plant. It means 'You are my inspiration'.'

'Is it a flower?'

'No. It's definitely a plant.'

I turn away. John turns with me. We're headed in the same direction. We've finished our conversation and now we're walking side by side. I can't speed up because my knees won't let me. I can't slow down because I don't have time. Ten minutes later we go our separate ways, and I know how to build a conservatory.

Note: Dispose of gloves, coat and balaclava. Bonfire. Note end.

Reverend Benjamin Christopher Gregory moved to Thailand eighteen months ago. He was marrying a young couple when he broke down in tears and had to be escorted from the altar. He came back minutes later, walked up to the best man and head-butted him square between the eyes. Soon after, someone sprayed graffiti across the side of his house and a picture appeared in the local newspaper of him sat on his doorstep, smoking a cigar and drinking whiskey from the bottle. He had bright red paint behind him, giant letters on a white pebbledash wall. It read, 'arsehole'. One word, no hyphen.

He was replaced by Judy. That's what we call her. If you try to call her anything else she stops you and says, 'Just call me Judy, that'll be fine'. Some older members of the congregation objected to her appointment because she cancelled Reverend Michael's day trip to the theme park. And because she's a woman. Some of them stopped attending Mass. One of them made a leaflet. Jesus not Judy.

Judy says hello to every single person as they enter the church. It's something she likes to do. Even if it means everyone has to turn and glare disapprovingly at the latecomer. It's ten thirty-three, I'm stood outside the church and Judy's already started. I can hear her through the thick wooden door as I twist the metal handle and step inside, take its weight as I close it. The door makes no sound. The congregation are facing the other way. Maybe she won't see me.

'A latecomer! Good morning, Gordon. Sit yourself down.' The sound of heads turning and elbows in coats rubbing against one another. The creak of handbags clutched in

74

laps. And I look up at Judy standing behind the pulpit, several feet above the rest of us. I can't shout back and ask her how her week's been, so I nod and attempt a smile, which she misses completely because she's back to what she was saying before I rudely interrupted. I find a seat at the back near the door.

'And today is a special day. We add to our normal service, the welcoming of a new life into our world. We're here to celebrate, in the name of our Lord Jesus Christ, the baptism of baby Matthew Alan. He was born just two months ago, a wonderful gift in this new year. We welcome his mother, Tracey, and his loving family.'

Tracey stands up, waves her hands and shouts, 'Hiya everyone.' She's wearing a denim miniskirt. She can't be more than sixteen. She looks like a child.

'But first I'd like to tell you about last Tuesday. You might have noticed this delightful scarf I have around my shoulders. Well, I had the pleasure of spending some time this week with the young children of St. Mary's Junior School. I talked to them about many things, including the importance of love. Love for God. Love for the family. Love for one another. And when I left, they gave me this scarf. It has its own unique design created by the children of St. Mary's, especially for me. If you look here, you can see the sunshine with its rays bursting forth. And below it, this beautiful red car. Isn't it just wonderful?'

A chorus of 'oohs'. A chorus of 'aahs'. And an, 'Isn't it lovely, Maureen.'

'And over here, there's a boat sailing on a bright blue sea. There, just by my shoulder. And if I turn around, you'll see a giant space rocket on my back.'

Judy turns to show us the rest of her scarf. I can just about make out the rocket. It has two curved areas at the base, which make it look like it's coming up through a cloud. It looks like men's parts.

'Can you see it at the back?' says Judy.

There's no commotion. No-one says a thing. They just sit there. Judy stretches her hand over her shoulder. She points at the rocket. 'Isn't it just fantastic?' she says.

It definitely looks like parts. And in a place of worship.

★ ★ ★

Baby Matthew Alan is christened. Tracey has chosen a hymn for us to sing at the end of the ceremony. 'All Things Bright and Beautiful', or as she calls it, 'All Creatures Big and Small'. Judy stands at the front and leads the

76

way while two elderly women walk between the aisles with a collection bucket. They shake it to make it rattle, which would be illegal if they were in the street. When they get to me they stop, look up and wait. I keep singing, put my hand in the bucket and avoid eye contact. I tap the side as I take my hand out again. It makes a noise that sounds like I've put money in. They thank me very much. Keep on rattling. Like Don Donald's pockets.

Judy brings Mass to a close and stands by the door. She likes to say goodbye as well as hello. I was last in and I'm first out. She stops me with the usual sympathetic smile. A newly-christened baby is wailing somewhere behind me.

'Glad you could make it, Gordon. How are you?'

'I'm well, thank you.'

'I saw Doctor Morris yesterday. I was picking up my mother's tablets. He says you're in good health.'

'Did he?'

'Yes, I was asking after you. He says you're keeping on top of things.'

'Well, that's very kind of you both.'

There's a hundred people and a screaming child behind me. I'm keeping them from leaving and I'm hogging Judy. Some of them are breathing down my neck. Literally.

'How's Georgina?'

And now I'm not talking. Everyone wants to know why Gordon's not talking. Who does he think he is? Why, when Judy's asked him a question, is he standing in silence, staring into space? If he doesn't want to answer the question, he could at least do the honest thing and change the subject. They're right. I should change the subject.

'The rocket's not a rocket. It's a penis.'

The noise behind me disappears. The church is silent again. Even the baby stops crying. A woman next to me puts her hands over her daughter's ears. Judy looks straight at me. For a few seconds she says nothing. I have no regrets.

'Gordon, would you like me to visit you at home?'

'You don't have to do that.'

'How about next week? Or the week after?'

'Honestly, there's no need.'

'I'll just come round for a chat, I think. That's what I'll do.'

She moves on to the next person, the noise starts up again and I shuffle outside. The sky is a deep, dull grey. It looks like it's been raining.

Gratuity

It's Wednesday afternoon, three days since 'The Rocket Incident'. Judy is yet to visit. I've been looking out for her, preparing the house to make it look like no-one's in. Church people have a tendency to wander into people's homes without permission. I keep the windows shut during the day and use the power-cut candles at night. It's just gone noon. Angelica has been to collect her newspapers, Benny has gone to school and Morris Webster stood at his window for a while. He put his hand on the glass and looked up at the sky, as if longing for rain. He was there for eleven minutes and thirty-four seconds. Then he disappeared. I made notes on it all. He'll need a cloth to wipe his fingerprints. Now, I'm sat on the chair next to the bed in Georgina's room. I'm preparing another bath. I roll my sleeve and put my arm in the washing-up bowl.

Note: Use bath thermometer. Temperature should not be higher than 115 degrees F, 46 degrees C. Help remove clothes and cover with blanket. Keep warm and give privacy. Note end.

I reach under the bed and pull out my shoebox. This is where I keep my supplies. Disposable gloves. Bath towel and flannel. Soap, powder, lotion, deodorant, toothbrush and toothpaste. Half an hour ago, I turned on the portable radiator to heat the room. It makes the air smell slightly burnt. I pull on a pair of gloves. They are transparent and tight on my hands. I have to clasp them together to push my fingers into the ends.

Georgina is naked and sleeping. I undressed her fifteen minutes ago, when the room began to get warm. I open my manual at the right page, place it on the bedside table and prop it against the wall. I put the flannel in the water, wet it without soap and squeeze to rinse. I gently wipe her eyelids and dry them with a towel. I do it from the inside corner to the outside corner. I use soap to wash her ears and neck. A slice of winter sunlight comes between the gap in the curtains and creeps across her face. I have to stop myself from counting the wrinkles between her mouth and nose. I have to ignore the line of dust caught in the light, settling on her lips. I put the towel under her arms as I wash them and I hold her hand when I clean her palms and between her fingers. I dry thoroughly. Especially the hair under her armpits, and the skin under her breasts. I fold the blanket down so I can wash, rinse and dry her chest and stomach. When I finish, I fold it back again and lift it from the bottom to do her legs, feet and toes. I shove the towel under her knees. Wash, rinse and dry.

This used to be a team effort. We used to do this together. I pick up the basin, walk to the bathroom and pour the dirty water into the sink. She would've shouted, 'Don't waste it. You can use that for your tea'. I walk back to the bedroom, dig my heels against the wall and use all my weight to push Georgina onto her side. She would've said, 'I can do that, you be careful of your back'. I use fresh water to wash, rinse and dry her back, buttocks and shoulders. 'Give us a rub while you're there', she would've said. I smear lotion over the open sores on her bare skin. She says nothing.

The last area to wash is the groin. I put a new pair of gloves on. I'm supposed to ask Georgina to lift her buttocks for me, but she's far too tired so instead I have to move her myself and put a towel under her at the same time. I can hear someone laughing outside. It sounds like a woman. Can I see through the curtains? I should ignore it. I hold Georgina's knee, spread her legs and jar them open with my shoulder. What if it's Angelica? With one hand I separate the labia. With the other I wash from front to back with the soapy flannel. I rinse then dry the area with the corner of the towel. More laughter. It's the only sound to get through the double glazing. I walk to the window. I was right. It's Angelica. There's a car parked outside her house. It's red apart from the driver's side door, which is green and looks like it used to belong to a different vehicle. Angelica is on the pavement, smoking a cigarette and smiling. Benny's on his knees at the back of the car. He's scrubbing a hubcap with a dirty sponge. I can't tell what he's saying, but I can hear Angelica laughing and I can see her shifting her weight from one leg to the other. I can trace the outline of her hips. This morning, when she collected her newspapers, she wore the same fluffy-cuffed coat as last week and a pair of jeans. I look at her now, hours later. She's taken her coat off and applied pink nail varnish. There's a gap between her jeans and t-shirt and I can see her skin. Benny dips his sponge into a bucket of water. He's naked from the waist up, like he is when he's painting. Angelica's arms are folded. They keep her stomach warm and her breasts together. If it weren't for the frost on the lawn behind them, you'd never believe it was winter. I can't imagine how cold they are.

There's a dull thud behind me. It takes me by surprise. Georgina has fallen onto her front. She's also fallen on top of the towel and pushed the blanket onto the floor. She's face down on the bed, completely naked and still asleep. It takes me nearly ten minutes to get the towel from underneath her, turn her onto her back and put her nightdress on. I have to sit on the chair to catch my breath. I hold her hand and imagine her squeezing mine. 'It'll be all right,' she would've said.

I go back to the window. Benny is pointing at the car and forcing his chest out. They stand too close when they talk. Angelica puts her hand into her jeans pocket, pulls out a banknote and gives it to Benny. Then they stop talking, look up at my window and stare at me, just for a few seconds. I stay exactly where I am. I'm not worried. There's no way they can know that I'm here. I've been watching far too long.

Heresy

John Bonsall's skip has disappeared. It's been replaced with a new one that has the letters 'NF' spray painted down the side. It's already half full. I'm behind the curtain with my breakfast. Kipling's on my lap and I'm resting my plate on his back. He's very sick. Too ill to go anywhere. It's Monday morning and the street is empty. Yesterday, I didn't go to church. A hot air balloon is rising in the distance behind the houses. Red with black polka dots, like a giant ladybird. I watch it climb into the clouds. It must have taken off from Blackheart Wood. Or where Blackheart Wood used to be, before they mined it in the 70s. It took twelve years to get the coal out. Now the trees have been replanted and the council use it for carnivals and car rallies. The cricket club play their home games in a clearing in the middle.

A car drives into the street and swerves round the tree in the road. It gets so far, does a three-point turn and drives back again. This happens a lot. Cressington Vale is one street down from a main road. The car slows as it goes back past the tree and the driver flicks a

V-sign. I finish my toast and put the plate on the floor. Kipling is making my legs ache, so I pick him up and drop him next to the plate. He sleeps throughout. Another balloon appears in the sky. This one's shaped like a hammer. It looks like it's chasing the ladybird. I reach for my pen and notepad, start to make a list.

Nine balloons take off in forty-five minutes. I've been watching the street as I've counted them. I've written down shapes and sizes. Still, nothing is happening. I decide to go downstairs and make a cup of tea. As I stand up, another car drives into the street. No, it's the same car. Big, black and expensive. The driver uses just one finger this time as he drives past the tree. And there's someone in the passenger seat who wasn't there before. The car stops opposite my house. Outside Angelica's. I reach for my file labelled 'Suspicious behaviour', but before I can take it from the shelf I hear the kitchen door opening downstairs. Someone's in the house. Someone is downstairs and they are in the house. Kipling knows it. He's awake and looking up at me. He's shaking. I reach under the bed and pull out my billiard cue case. It's covered in dust. I open it, take out the cue and start screwing the ends together. It seems to take forever. I can hear the intruder walking around downstairs. The floorboards in the hall are squeaking and I can feel a draught coming up because the back door is open. I can smell the lemon cake I baked last night. Why didn't I lock the door? I'm sure I locked the door. Kipling jumps onto the bed and squeezes himself between the pillows.

'Is there anybody in? I'm a burglar!'

I knew it. It was only a matter of time. They should never have cancelled the neighbourhood watch. I grip the cue firmly and edge onto the landing. My back is tight to the wall as I creep downstairs. One at a time. Don't make a sound. I can hear them in the kitchen. They've put the kettle on. The cheek of it. What sort of burglar makes themselves at home? I stand at the bottom of the stairs. I hold the cue close to my body. I get chalk on the tip of my nose. It will have to wait. There's a criminal on the other side of this door.

I take a deep breath.

Hold the cue in attack position.

Enter the kitchen.

The burglar is bent over the kitchen table with their back to me. I can't stop myself. My arms have taken over and I'm bringing the cue down over their head. It's going to hit them just above the neck and it's probably going to knock them out. It may even kill them. And they deserve it. Just before the cue makes impact, the burglar turns around. It's a woman. No, it's not a woman, it's Judy. I'm about to murder a reverend.

Note: Time taken from point of entry to critical strike = 35 seconds. Too slow. Buy new slippers. Change locks. Note end.

There is silence. Slowly, I open my eyes. Judy's in a heap on the floor with half a billiard cue by her head. The other half is still in my hands and broken at the handle. I might be able to use it as a dibber. I can't believe there's no blood.

'You stupid fucking man!'

'Oh God, I'm sorry.'

'What the hell were you thinking?'

'I didn't mean to hit you.'

'You hit the shitting table.'

'There's no need to swear.'

'You've just tried to smash me over the head with a snooker cue, Gordon.'

'It's a billiard cue and you're a woman of the church.'

'Not when someone nearly kills me.'

'How did you get in?'

'The door was unlocked.'

'Why didn't you knock?'

'I knocked when I came in. And I shouted!'

'You said you were a burglar.'

'And do you think that's what they do? Do you walk into buildings and tell everyone you're an idiot?'

'No, I don't.'

'Well, you should.' I hold out my hand to help her up. She ignores it, puts her elbow on one of the chairs and helps herself up. I can hear the kettle boiling. I should offer her a cup of tea.

'Would you like . . . '

'No, thank you. I came to see Georgina. I was also going to ask if you were feeling all right, but frankly, you seem full of energy.'

'Georgina's not here.'

'She's not here?'

'No, she's spending some time at my parents.'

'Your parents?'

'Yes.'

'Well, that's super. Fantastic.'

'Yes.'

'I thought she might've had something of a relapse. We've not seen her since Christmas.'

'She's fine.'

'Her recovery has been astounding.'

'A miracle.'

'A miracle indeed, Gordon.' Judy is Judy again. She's stopped swearing.

'Is there anything else?'

'I also wondered why you missed Mass yesterday.'

'I didn't miss Mass.'

'No?

'No.'

'Well, I didn't see you in church, Gordon.'

'I didn't see you, either.'

'You didn't see me?'

'No.'

'I don't understand.'

'Me neither.' She looks me up and down. Turns her nose up.

'This is ridiculous. Are you sure you're okay? First you try and hit me over the head with a snooker cue, and now you're talking gibberish.'

'It's a billiard cue. Was a billiard cue.'

'I don't care what it is. Tell me how you are.'

'I'm okay.' She looks at me, puts her hands on her hips. I think she's going to swear again. 'Are you okay?'

'I'm okay and I'm leaving. Tell Georgina, I'm glad she's feeling better.'

'I will.'

'And Gordon?'

'Yes, Judy?'

'I suggest you visit the surgery. I think you need to see someone. I know it's not been easy.'

'Where are you going?'

'I'm going home.'

'That's the back garden.'

'I'll climb over the wall and into Mrs Tyson's garden. It's quicker.'

'Mrs Tyson?'

'She lives behind you. She's ninety-five next month. She'll never know I was there.' Judy walks away from me. She gets halfway down the garden and turns around.

'Gordon, don't tell anyone I swore.'

'Twice.'

'Don't tell them I swore at all.'

She hitches her skirt up and tucks it into what looks like a pair of red and white striped football socks. Then, she puts one foot in the middle of the wall, grabs one of the coping stones and hauls herself into Mrs Tyson's rhododendron bush. She shouts 'Bollocks' at the top of her voice. I close the door and pick up the other half of the cue. It's the first time I've used it since Georgina first got ill. I throw it straight in the bin. I walk back upstairs to the spare room and look through the window. The balloons are gone. So is the car. I wait for over an hour. It doesn't reappear and I need the toilet. I walk past Georgina's room and look through the gap in the door. Kipling's with her. He's managed to squeeze his head between the mattress and her armpit. His ribs are moving up and down as he sleeps. It looks like she's cuddling him, but her eyelids are still. She has no idea that he's there.

Heroes

Kipling is eighty-five dog years old. A brown and white Springer spaniel with large floppy ears, like a pair of socks draped over his head. He arrived just two days before Georgina told me she wanted us to stop trying for children. It never felt like a coincidence. We'd wanted children for so many years. I'd make charts and graphs and Georgina would attach them to the fridge with magnets. We called them our baby papers. She kept me informed and I kept them up to date. On the day we stopped trying, Kipling climbed onto the kitchen table, leapt across the room and pulled them off with his teeth. He'd only been with us a week. I collected the torn pieces of paper and put them in the bin. We never spoke about children again. We had Kipling. That's all that mattered. He would have to do.

I remember the day Georgina brought him home. I arrived back from work one day to find him sat in my chair, drinking from my favourite mug.

'Look what I've found,' she said.

'That's my best mug.'

'Isn't he lovely?'

'Why did you have to use my mug?'

'Shut up, Gordon. What shall we call him?'

'How can you find a dog?'

'He was tied to a lamppost.'

'You stole him?'

'No I didn't steal him. Someone abandoned him.'

'Well, we can't keep him.'

'Of course we can keep him.'

'That dog is not staying in this house.'

'Get yourself a drink and sit down. What shall we call him?'

'Are you sure that it's a him? We don't want hundreds of them.'

I put my hand out to stroke him. He sat bolt upright and looked me straight in the eye. We froze for a second, stared at each other. Then he jumped up and dug his teeth into the sleeve of my coat. I screamed and snatched my arm away. Kipling came with it. I ran around the room, shaking my limbs to try and get him off. It was impossible. Eventually, I stopped. Broken like a horse. Kipling hung with his legs in the air and his eyes fixed on mine. I walked to the kitchen and used my free hand to put the kettle on.

* * *

We called him Kipling after he ate too many cakes and threw up on our duvet. Before that he was called Bobby, but we'd only had him a month and Georgina wanted to change it. She said Bobby was boring. Too human-sounding. So Bobby became Kipling. Later, Georgina called him Super Kipling. He had a blue and yellow jumper with a red 'K' knitted into the front. It was given to him by the wife of the man he saved from drowning. We were out walking by the reservoir. The man had been fishing and lost his balance casting. He was struggling to keep his head above water. His wife stood on the bank, holding a sandwich and shouting. Georgina let go of my hand and started running towards them, but she was overtaken by Kipling. He leapt into the water and dragged the man back to shore.

Howard and Beverley Mainwairing, they were called. Georgina made me take them both to casualty. I had to walk back home and get the car. It turned out Georgina and Howard had been at school together when they were kids. A fortnight later they came to the house with a bottle of wine and Kipling's jumper. Georgina loved it. She made him wear it when she took him out for a walk, even in summer. He used to come back panting. 'He's red hot,' I used to tell her.

'That jumper's going to kill him'. But it made no difference, she made him wear it anyway. She was so proud. I remember the look he used to give me when he saw it coming out of the drawer. He wished he'd let poor Howard drown.

⋆ ⋆ ⋆

Kipling hasn't been the same since Georgina's first stroke. He always knew that something was wrong. When Georgina was at her worst, he spent most of his time with Don. They did everything together. Biscuits, walks and bath times. Don said it saved on water. Like when he uses Fairy Liquid instead of bubble bath, soap and shampoo. Three in one. Everyone knows when Don's had a bath. A huge cloud of suds and foam runs from his drain to the pavement and into the street. Kipling loved living there. He liked the peace and quiet. He got sick of all the people coming to our house. The strangers with their briefcases and their cups of tea in the kitchen. He'd often make a break for it. Or at least he did before he got ill. I'd be in the garden with the front door open. He'd creep slowly up the path, through the gate and over to Don's house. I'd let him think that I hadn't noticed, go and fetch him at the end of the day. 'How's he been?' I'd say to Don. 'No problem, Gordon. No bother at all. Just let me know if there's anything else that I can do.'

The truth is, I never did let Don know when something needed doing, because I didn't have to. He was always there regardless. Always available and always willing to help. He'd wash my car and cut the lawn. He'd do odd jobs around the house. Anything to keep himself busy and make my life easier. The one thing that he didn't do was help me care for Georgina. Not directly. He never offered either, because he knew I'd never let him. On Tuesdays and Thursdays Don would wait until she'd gone to bed and then he'd come over. We'd spend the rest of the evening together. Georgina would be exhausted by half past seven. Worn out by her exercises and the need to keep going, the struggle to adjust to our new way of living. When she was ready, I'd help her upstairs and into her pyjamas. We'd stand at the bathroom sink and clean her teeth together, my hand round hers to help her hold the toothbrush. Then I'd tuck her into bed, kiss her goodnight and wait for Don to arrive.

'Evening Gordon.' He'd step into the

house, take off his coat and hang it over the radiator in the hall. 'Warm it up for the return journey,' he'd say.

'Tea, Don?'

'Yes please.'

'How many sugars?'

'What day is it? Tuesday. Just the one thank you.'

'Pickled onion?'

'Yes please.'

'I'll bring it through when it's ready. Sit yourself down in there.'

We'd sit in the living room and talk like we did when we were young. He'd tell me about his wife that barely was and we'd laugh about it together. They were the same stories he'd been telling me for thirty years. The same characters with the same punch lines. And I didn't mind listening, because it was better than being on my own. Occasionally, Don would try to talk about Georgina. He'd ask me how I was coping and if I'd thought about taking a break, going somewhere nice, speaking to my mother and father. I'd change the subject or pretend I didn't understand what he was getting at.

Mostly I didn't mind him asking, but sometimes my frustration got the better of me. My anger at what had happened. At the speed of Georgina's progress. Don would try to reassure me that things would eventually get better, but that would only make things worse. I'd tell him not to be so patronising. Not to pretend that things weren't as bad as they were. He absorbed my words again and again. He would always understand. He would never complain. I don't know what I would have done without him.

Inkling

It rained on our wedding day. Georgina ran from the taxi to the church. Her dress dragged across the floor, her heels flicked dirty water up her back. She looked beautiful. My parents and Georgina's mother sat behind us on the front row. My father wore a grey cardigan with pink stripes across the chest and a pink shirt underneath. Georgina told him he couldn't wear a suit because he always wore a suit. She said pink was the theme. He wasn't happy about it, although the cardigan wrapped nicely round his arm, which he'd broken falling from his lorry the week before.

We had the reception at the community centre, the same place we'd said goodbye to Georgina's father, just two years previous. It was almost identical. The same people and the same drinks. The same music by the same DJ. Only the buffet was different. My mother prepared it herself. She put the tables up and the food out. No-one was allowed to go near. She knew where everything needed to be, right down to the last sausage on a stick. My father tried to steal a slice of quiche before the buffet opened. But she'd been watching like a hawk and punched him in the ribs before his fingers reached the plate.

Georgina sat on my knee in the corner of the room. She had her arm around my neck and her hand on my cheek. We watched her mother with the DJ again, dragging him to the floor and forcing him to dance with her. She grabbed the back of his head and hauled him close, jammed it between her neck and her shoulder. Georgina laughed out loud. 'Look at her,' she said. 'I wish my Dad could see her now.' And she pointed to her mother's hands as they worked their way down the DJ's back and clawed his buttocks.

The music stopped at midnight. I watched my mother and father from the car park as I loaded the boot with wedding gifts and uneaten sandwiches. They were slow dancing to Frank Sinatra, the last song of the night. Georgina was clearing up plates and thanking the bar staff. She'd taken off her dress and hung it over a radiator. It was still damp at the bottom but she'd packed a pair of trousers, just in case. I listened to the song fade out and watched my mother kiss my father on the cheek. She helped him put his cardigan on. Then he walked to the fire exit, opened the door and lit a cigarette. I held my hand up and waved to him.

'All right, Son?' he said, stepping down from the doorway into darkness. He disappeared until I caught the orange glow of his cigarette. His outline against the trees.

'Thanks for today, Dad.'

'Don't thank me, thank your wife. You're lucky someone will have you.'

We both laughed. He turned and sat on the bonnet of the car. He took a long drag of his cigarette. It glowed bright again. Then he threw it on the floor and stamped it out. He walked over to me.

'I'm sorry her Dad couldn't be here,' I said.

'He's here somewhere. He was a good man. I know he's here somewhere.'

'You think?'

'You know I do. And so should you. He's with the Lord, but he's still watching over us. They both are.'

'I know. I didn't mean that.'

'What did you mean?'

'You know what people say about him.'

I barely finished my sentence before I felt my father's hand across my cheek. I stumbled, fell to one knee, stood back up immediately. I touched my face with the back of my wrist. I said nothing.

'He was a good man.'

'Yes, Dad. I know he was.'

I picked the last gift off the floor and slid it onto the parcel shelf. My father reached up and shut the boot. He put his hand on my shoulder and smiled at me, his breath still fresh with smoke.

'You've got a good one there,' he said. 'Make sure you look after her.'

* * *

My father sat in the front with Georgina's dress on his lap while my mother drove. He used his non-broken arm to smoke out the passenger seat window. I sat squashed between Georgina and her mother in the back. The smell of almost-stale sandwiches wafting in from the boot. Corned beef and mustard. My father's pickled onions.

'Are you sure they're not leaking?' I said.

'Those jars don't leak,' said my father.

'They'd better not leak on my presents,' said Georgina.

'Your presents?' I said.

My father turned round in his seat, 'Those jars are watertight.'

Georgina laughed and squeezed my arm, 'Are they vinegar tight though?' My father laughed with her and winked. My mother cleared her throat. 'It doesn't matter how tight they are, they won't stop the smell,' she said. 'It's all right for you. You don't have to live with it.'

'Not anymore,' I said.

We'd moved into our new house the weekend before the wedding. It meant we had to delay our honeymoon for six months. We didn't mind though. We'd found the house we'd been looking for. The house we wanted. Number eighteen, Cressington Vale. Kitchen, bathroom, living room. Two bedrooms. One master and one spare for when guests came, or if we ever had children. Two gardens but no garage. A spacious loft. It would be hard work. But it would be worth it. It would be perfect. We'd have to decorate. Use boxes for chairs until we found our own furniture. Keep frozen food in Don Donald's freezer. Our new neighbour. The one whose wife just left him. He had plenty of space.

'Next left,' said my father.

'I know where I'm going,' my mother replied.

She pulled the car into Georgina's street. Georgina's old street. We came to a stop outside what was now just her mother's house. My father stepped out the car and opened the back door. My mother put the handbrake on and took her feet from the pedals. She left the engine running. Mary had fallen asleep on my shoulder. I dug my elbow into her ribs to wake her up.

'We're home,' Georgina said. 'Gordon's Dad's going to walk you to the door.'

'Thanks for all your help,' I said.

'Are you coming in?'

'No Mum. We're going home.'

'Home? You've only been there a week.'

'It's been such a long day. We'll see you tomorrow.'

'It's not your home yet.'

'You can help us strip the wallpaper if you like, Mary.'

My father grabbed her forearm and helped her out of the car. He bent down, looked through the open window and said, 'I'll be back in a minute.' Georgina's mother turned and waved as he put his foot on the garden gate, pushed it open with his heel. We waved back at her. 'Sleep tight,' my mother shouted as they wandered down the path towards the house. Georgina's mother opened her bag, shoved her hand inside and started searching for her keys. After thirty seconds my father snatched the bag and started searching for them himself. After another minute, he pulled them out and unlocked the front door. He opened it, switched the light on in the hall. We watched them go inside. The door closed slowly and of its own accord. The springs too tight on its hinges.

'Is she all right?' I said.

'She'll be fine,' said Georgina. 'She's just drunk.'

'Are you sure?'

'I'm sure.'

'She takes up a lot of room.'

'I know, I could hardly breathe.'

My mother put her elbow on the edge of her seat and used it to turn herself around. 'Don't be cheeky, you two,' she said. 'You might be old enough to get married, but you're not too old . . . ' and then she stopped. 'Mary's lost one of her earrings.'

'Where?' I said.

'Right next to you.'

'Where?'

'There.'

'What do you mean, 'there'? I can't see it.'

'It's by your leg.'

'Which leg?'

'That leg.'

'This leg?'

'No, the other leg.'

Georgina reached over, picked up the earring and held it to the window. It caught the light from the streetlamp. 'She's right,' said Georgina. 'Can you see the other one?' I ran my hand across the upholstery, felt a sharp pain in my thumb and yelped. 'It's here,' I said.

'That was lucky. Why don't you run in and give them to her now?'

'I'm not running.'

'You know what I mean.'

I pulled the earring out of my thumb and checked for blood. Georgina gave me the other earring. I put them in my pocket, stepped from the car and walked towards the house. 'Tell your Dad to hurry up while you're there,' I heard my mother shout. The rain had stopped but the lawn was soaked. I grabbed my trousers at the knee and lifted them above my ankles, opened the front door with my shoulder. It closed behind me as I walked through the hall towards the kitchen. The only room with a light on. I passed the entrance to the living room, thought about Georgina's father sat drinking in his comfy chair. Then I heard the sound of someone laughing. Or crying. Georgina's mother in the kitchen. I stopped. I stood still. The door was half open, half closed, but wide enough for me to peer through the gap between the door and the frame. I edged closer. My father had his back to me. Georgina's mother's face buried in his chest. She was definitely laughing. Or crying. She had her arms around him and her hands on his shoulder blades. I could see a bottle of wine and a packet of cereal on the table. The Sunday dinner table. My father had one hand on her hip, the other inside his sling and pink cardigan. I watched Georgina's mother's fingers slide down his back.

'I've got your earrings, Mary,' I said, looking away, pushing the door open, walking into the kitchen. They let go of each other. Stood side by side.

'Gordon,' my father said. 'Where's your mother?'

'She wants you to hurry up. You left your earrings in the car.'

'Oh, thank you,' said Mary. 'I hadn't noticed.'

'They cut my finger.'

'Could you put them on the table?'

'Mum says the engine's running.'

I turned and walked back down the hallway. 'Right, we might see you tomorrow then?' I heard my father say, 'We'll let ourselves out.' And then he followed me through the door and into the garden. He jogged to catch me up. He put his arm around my shoulders. We walked across the wet lawn together. He kissed me on the back of the head and waved at my mother and Georgina in the car. He told me it had been a beautiful day. A wonderful wedding.

Inhibitions

Unfortunately, Kipling has diarrhoea again. Sometimes there's nothing wrong with him. We get up, I take him for his walk and he spends the rest of the day by the radiator. Everything's normal. On other days, he refuses to leave the house. He sits shaking by the bathroom door and loses control of his bowels. I'm sitting in the surgery waiting room with my legs apart and a cardboard box on my knee. It was easy to get Kipling inside the box. When he's not shaking, he's sleeping. I've poked holes in the bottom with a fork so he can breathe. No-one suspects a thing. I've also checked my files. It's half past three. Angelica should be here any minute. I spoke to her yesterday. I stood in the garden on purpose, waiting for her to leave the house. I asked her what her plans were. She told me she would be here. We're becoming friends. My appointment is at four, but I arrived an hour ago. I didn't want to miss her.

Doctor Jonathan Morris has received an official warning for repeatedly leaving his intercom on during consultations. Last week, a man came in to see him with a suspected hernia and someone made a complaint to the receptionist. Now they've got rid of the intercom system completely. It's been replaced by an electronic sign that sits above the door-to-the-corridor-that-leads-to-the-doctor. Patients' names scroll across in a series of red dots that make up letters. They're followed by the name of the doctor they're here to see. If someone misses their name, they drop a place in the queue. I preferred the intercom.

The horseshoe of seats is full. I'm sat with my legs apart for two reasons. First, it means the air can get to the holes in the bottom of Kipling's box. And second, so I take up more room on the seat. When Angelica gets here she'll have nowhere to sit. That is, she'll have nowhere to sit unless I close my legs and make some space for her. She's coming now. I can tell by the shape of her shoulders through the frosted glass of the surgery door. It's like looking through her bathroom window.

'Hello Gordon,' she says. I shuffle up and she sits next to me.

'Hello.'

'You're here again?'

'And so are you.'

'What's in the box?'

'I can't really say.'

'Well, that's intriguing.'

'Promise you won't tell?'

'Probably, yes. What is it?'

If possible, I speak to Angelica every day. Sometimes, she doesn't come out of her house, but I can usually orchestrate a chance meeting by referring to her file. We get on well. She does most of the talking.

I lean over and whisper, 'It's Kipling.'

'Kipling the dog?'

'Of course.'

'You shouldn't bring him in here.'

'I know. It's okay though. I'm taking him to see Doctor Morris.'

'You need a vet not a doctor. What's wrong with him? He's not still shitting everywhere is he?'

Angelica has a foul mouth, there's no doubt about it. I bring out the worst in her. I swore when we first met. She remembers. She thinks I'm the type of person who swears. I don't care. She has a wonderful smirk on her face. This is excellent.

'Angelica, do you know what he did this morning?'

'I've no idea.'

'He shit in my slippers.'

Note: Gift ideas for Angelica. Something small. Something practical. Something that I know she likes. Refer to files. Note end.

We've been chatting for nearly eight minutes. My name goes past on the electronic sign. I ignore it. Angelica didn't see as she was busy talking. We've been together long enough for her perfume to attach itself to my clothes. I'll be able to smell it for the rest of the day.

'You've got a car?' I ask her.

'Oh, you've seen it then?'

'Only from a distance.'

'Yes, well it's very old, but it'll do the job.'

'As long as it gets you from A to B.'

'Let's hope so.'

Why has my name scrolled past again? They never show the same name twice. I look across at the receptionist. She's glaring at me. I look back at the electronic sign. It's on repeat.

'Why was Benny washing it?'

'I'm sorry?'

'I saw Benny washing your car.'

'I asked him to.'

'Even though I told you about the stealing?'

'I mentioned that to him actually. He laughed.'

'Did he?'

'Yes, but I didn't tell him that it was you who told me.'

'Okay,' I say, more feebly than I mean to.

Angelica folds her arms and looks up at the sign.

'Gordon, your name's been flashing for a while now. I think you'd better go in.'

★ ★ ★

Doctor Morris has his back to me. His hands are on his head and he's staring out the window. Kipling is asleep on his desk. He turns around. I can see his sweat patches.

'For the last time, I cannot examine — or treat — your dog.'

'It won't take a minute.'

'I can't do it. And even if I could, I wouldn't know how to. I'm a doctor. A human doctor. I am not a veterinary nurse or person. I can't believe you brought him in here, Gordon. I really can't.'

'I thought you could help.'

'Why? Why did you think I'd be able to help?'

'Aren't vets expensive?'

'I don't know. I've no idea if vets are expensive. Do you want to know why? It's because I'm a doctor. I'm not a vet.'

He sits down behind his desk. I lift Kipling and put him back in the box. I close the lid. It was stupid of me to bring him here. There's nothing wrong with him. He'll be fine.

Doctor Morris moves his chair in front of the notice board. I can read the posters over his shoulder.

Teenage pregnancy: Five top tips for parents.

'I should apologise, Gordon. I shouldn't lose my temper like that. It's unprofessional. However, there's nothing I can do for your dog. Perhaps you should take him to see someone else.'

Angelica will be sitting here soon. She might even be next. I wonder what she's here for. I should ask her. She probably calls him Jonathan. I can see it now. She'll fold her arms to make her cleavage creep towards her chin. Like she does with Benny.

1. Be clear about your own sexual values and attitudes.

She'll lean backwards in her seat and flick her ponytail. He'll offer her a drink. He has coffee in a drawer under his desk. For special occasions.

2. Supervise and monitor your children and adolescents.

'There's a veterinary clinic about fifteen miles away, Gordon. A friend of mine takes their cat. Let me see if I've got their number.'

3. Know your children's friends and families.

She'll drink his coffee and leave lipstick

113

marks on the rim of the mug. Some of the coffee will dribble down the outside. She'll lick it off with her tongue. He'll ask her to take her clothes off and make herself comfortable on the bed.

4. *Take a stand against your daughter dating a boy significantly older than she is; don't allow your son to develop an intense relationship with a much younger girl.*

She'll lie half naked while he rubs his hands together. A red mark wrapped around her back where her bra was too tight. Her stomach squeezing over the sides of her jeans. Jonathan's palms glistening as he holds them up to the strip lighting.

5. *Know what your children are watching, reading and listening to.*

Dripping with oil, he'll knead his fingers into her loose skin. She'll turn her head away from him, close her eyes and grip the sides of the bed. Then he'll scrape his nails down her spine, put his hands where he shouldn't. Like he did with that girl.

'Are you okay, Gordon?'

'Pardon?'

'Are you all right? You're not with me.'

'I'm here. I'm with you.'

'Listen, I didn't mean to upset you. I don't have the number with me, but I can get reception to ring you with it tomorrow. Okay?'

'That would be good. Thank you, Jonathan.'

'Jonathan? I've never been called that by a patient.'

'Sorry.'

'It's fine, I don't mind. Is there anything else?'

'Yes.'

'What is it?'

'I'd like everything checked. One of us needs to be well.'

It's thirty-three minutes past four. I've just got home. It's dark outside. I lift Kipling out of the box and put him next to his bowl. He goes straight to the radiator, lies down and closes his eyes. He is shaking already. I just need to keep an eye on him. If he doesn't want to walk in the morning, we won't walk. No pressure. I go upstairs to the spare room and take Angelica's file from the shelf. I transcribe our conversation in the waiting room. I remember every word. I take Kipling's file. It contains a plastic wallet with a picture inside that he painted himself. Georgina put his foot in a tin of emulsion when we decorated the living room. She used to keep the picture on the fridge. Now it's just a crinkled piece of paper with a magnolia paw print in the middle. You have to hold it to the light to see the change in colour.

I open Kipling's file and put my hand inside the wallet. I can feel the picture, his paw print on the paper, hard and brittle. I reach to the bottom, pull out a tiny folded jumper with a red 'K' on the front. Then I go downstairs, pick Kipling up and sit him on my knee. His ears prick at the sight of the jumper. He looks me straight in the eye. 'Don't worry. She's still sleeping,' I tell him. 'But she's getting better.'

Intimacy

It's Sunday again. I haven't been to Mass because I don't want to see Judy. This morning I spoke to Georgina and she almost spoke back. I'd been to the bathroom to get her medication, fill her glass with water and crush the tablets onto a saucer. I dipped my fingers into the water and turned to sprinkle droplets on her forehead. But she was awake. Her eyes were open. One eye more than the other, but they were open. I sat on the chair by the bed. Then I stood up and sat on the bed itself. I ran my wet fingers across her brow and down her cheek. I held her good hand. She closed her eyes slowly. Opened them again. 'Good morning,' I whispered. 'Fancy a jog?' She smiled. Her mouth changed shape. Her cheekbones lifted, glistened in the light from the bedside lamp. The trace of water from my fingers on her skin. I tried to let go of her hand but her grip tightened. Her lips moved like she was trying to speak. 'It's all right,' I said. 'You've just woken up. Can you give me a squeeze?'

That's what we used to do. That was the system. I'd hold her hand and she'd let me

117

know what she wanted. What she was feeling. What she needed me to do. It meant we could communicate. It meant that she got better.

It was our code:

One squeeze = Where?
Two squeezes = What?
Three squeezes = Why?
Four squeezes = When?
Five squeezes = How?
Six squeezes = Who?
Stroke palm = Yes
Pinch finger = No

She looked up at me, squeezed my hand three times. She opened her mouth and pursed her lips. The bottom lip more than the top. Her teeth tight together. She pinched my finger. Squeezed my hand again. Three times, with barely any force. 'Mass? Of course I went. You were asleep,' I said. She moved her hand slowly, tried to pinch my finger. 'Honest. It was a short service, so I wasn't gone for long. Judy's father's taken a turn for the worse.' She closed her eyes again. For longer this time. 'Come on, wake up. You need to take your tablets.' I helped her to sit up in bed, supported the side that didn't work. Her stupid side, as she used to call it. Last week I put our wedding photos back in the manual.

We used to go through them together. The speech therapist said it might help. I'd say the names of friends and family members and ask Georgina to repeat them back to me. I never asked her to repeat my name because I couldn't face her getting it wrong. Or not remembering. I'm going to start going through them again with her soon. I'm going to use some other pictures too. I've been cutting them out of magazines and newspapers. People, objects, animals. Like the pictures the therapist used. I might laminate them.

I held the glass of water and helped Georgina take her tablets. She swallowed them at the second attempt. I wiped saliva from her chin and put the glass back on the bedside table. I put my hand back in hers. She's getting stronger. We're getting stronger. I felt it. She let go of my hand, turned it over and used her finger to write on my palm. Slowly, shaking, she carved invisible letters on my skin. TY = thank you. 'You're welcome,' I said. 'There's a yoghurt in the fridge.' She touched my palm again. One small soft stroke = yes. 'I'll fetch it in a minute. I need to do your exercises first.' Georgina closed her eyes, grimaced as much as her muscles allowed. I smiled and let go of her hand, before she could pinch my finger.

Job-hopping

Georgina has been asleep for most of the afternoon. It's three weeks since she had her second stroke and three weeks minus one day since Angelica arrived. I'm in the kitchen baking a sponge cake. I'm using a simple recipe. Just sponge, jam and cream, no icing. I don't have time to make anything else because I'm cooking for Georgina. We're going to eat together tonight. I'm going to put the fold-up picnic table by the side of her bed. I'm preparing mashed potatoes, carrots, cabbage and peas. Real ones, freshly prepared, not frozen or from a packet. I'm having mine with chicken and mushroom pie. Georgina's having hers liquidised. This morning, I used the manual to test her swallowing again. I told her I'd fetched the blender back down from the loft. I asked her if she thought she was ready. I held her hand. One stroke = yes.

I tell myself that she's improving because it's true. We know exactly what we are doing. We don't need anyone. This morning, I watched her fall asleep again after she'd taken her tablets and eaten her breakfast. I sat on the chair by the bed and thought about how much better she looked. How much movement she'd regained. I watched her eyelids fight to stay open, just for a few seconds. The trace of a smile. She'd been awake for two hours and twelve minutes. I wrote it down. She's sleeping less each day and soon she'll be able to try walking again. I've been studying the manual. I remember everything we went through. We've done this before and we can do it again. Tonight, when we've finished our dinner, if Georgina's not too tired, I'll ask her if she feels like noughts and crosses.

★   ★   ★

Georgina is still sleeping and I'm watching Angelica from behind the curtain. She's spent over forty-five minutes at her living room window, looking out towards the entrance to the street. I've opened another file. She keeps pressing her cheek against the glass, like she's expecting someone. Twenty minutes ago Don Donald pushed his wheelie bin to the end of his drive and stood next to it for a while, propped up by his elbow on the lid. He put his arm across his chest and arched his back. He was wearing a shirt, tie and pyjama bottoms. He looked old.

Now it's getting dark and curtains along Cressington Vale are closing. Angelica pulls hers shut and appears at her front door seconds later. She stands on the step, a silhouette against the light from the hallway behind her. She holds a cigarette in the air, her arm and hand bent into an L-shape. A sock puppet smoking. I look past her, along the hall and into the kitchen. I can see a figure standing at the sink. It's a man. He's washing plates and dishes. I can't see his face. Angelica finishes her cigarette and steps backwards into the house, closing the door. I continue to stare at her curtains. The reflection of the street in her window. It wasn't Benny. That would be impossible.

Note: Over six feet tall. Blue jeans with a red, long-sleeved shirt. Sleeves rolled up. Dark hair, no shoes but wearing socks. Young. Twenties. Possibly younger. All guestimates. Difficult to see. May have been wearing an apron. Note end.

My sponge cake has cooled. It's perfect. I cut a slice and place it in Kipling's bowl. He loves my sponge cake. He picks himself up from beneath the radiator, ambles over to the bowl and falls into a heap. He sniffs the cake while lying on his side. He twists his head so his

122

chin rests on the rim of the bowl. He falls asleep without eating. I put the rest of the cake on the table, grab Kipling's collar and drag him back to the radiator, where it's warm. He doesn't wake up. I'm taking him to the vets later this week. Jonathan didn't give me the number because the phone is disconnected. I unplugged it at the wall fifteen minutes after Georgina's stroke. But the surgery has our address. He could have put the number through the letterbox. He still let me down. Angelica gave me the number instead. She said I looked worried. I said I thought Kipling might still improve. She said I should get him seen to by someone who knows what they're doing. I went to the newsagents and picked up a new box. It used to contain packets of crisps and there's a hole in the side for your hand. Kipling's head will fit through perfectly.

The vegetables are ready. Overcooked to make them softer, easier to liquidise. I put my portion on a plate and put the plate in the oven to stop them going cold. I put Georgina's in the blender and check for lumps when I've finished. Then I check again, make sure for certain that there aren't any. I pour the liquid into a mug, pick some up with a spoon and watch it slide back into the mixture. It's thin enough for her to swallow. I take the plate out of the oven and put the chicken and mushroom pie next to the vegetables. I boil the kettle for the gravy. I put both the plate and mug on a tray and push the kitchen door open with my foot. Kipling opens his eyes, gets up from the radiator and stumbles after me. He'll sit by the end of the bed while we eat. Georgina will hold my hand, ask me if he's feeling any better. I'll lie and tell her he's going to be fine.

Jinxed

Georgina is a champion noughts and crosses player. She used to beat me all the time. We spent most of our honeymoon playing. We had a caravan overlooking the sea front, a narrow beach tapering out towards rocks and cliff tops either side, which we paid extra for. It rained all week, from start to finish. We spent most of our time indoors. The only time we went outside was to get the morning papers and a bottle of milk. Georgina's mother arrived on the fifth day. She'd arranged to spend the second weekend with us. Georgina had insisted.

'I can't believe the weather down here.'

'What's it like at home, Mum?'

'The sun's shining. I'd have been better off staying where I was.'

'You can go back if you want, Mary,' I said.

'Watch your mouth. I didn't ask to come, I was invited.'

'He's just pulling your leg. Ignore him. We're glad for the company. It's been like this since we got here. You must be hungry.'

Georgina stood up and walked from the living area to the kitchen. She started looking through the fridge. I picked up my pen and began ruling a new grid.

'Gordon, do you have to draw so many squares?' said her mother.

'I'm afraid so. It's too easy for her otherwise.'

'I'll never win any way. I don't see how it makes a difference.'

'You've only been here a few hours. She's been beating me all week. You can play me on my own later.'

★ ★ ★

'How about a sandwich, Mum?' Georgina shouted, from behind the fridge door. 'We've got ham, cheese, tomatoes and beef. You can have some of Gordon's Dad's pickled onions as well, if you like. And we've got half a pork pie.'

'I don't think those onions are ready yet,' I said. 'They might need to wait a few weeks.'

'There's nothing wrong with them. She can have them if she wants. The people that were in before us left a yoghurt at the back. It's still in date. Do you want that for pudding?'

'What flavour is it?' I said. 'I might have that.'

'Fruits of the forest, and no you won't. Mum, what do you want to eat?'

There was no answer. Georgina poked her head round the fridge door. I looked up from ruling my grid. Her mother was slouched on the sofa. She was staring into space.

'Mum, are you okay?'

'Yes, I think so.'

'Why, what's wrong?'

'I'm fine, it's just a little blurred.'

'What do you mean, blurred?'

'I think I need new glasses.'

'Are you all right?'

'I'm fine. I can see you.'

Georgina closed the fridge. She looked at me. I put down my pen and moved over to her mother. She tried to lift her arm for me to sit down, but could only drag it over the upholstery. I held her hand and squeezed her fingers.

'Can you feel that?'

'Of course I can. It's just pins and needles. Get on with the game. I had a sandwich on the coach. I'll not be hungry for an hour.'

That night, the rain faded to a drizzle. Georgina sat on the caravan steps listening to the waves crashing against the rocks. I poured us both a cup of tea and sat behind her with my arms around her shoulders. Her mother was in bed. We sat and stared into the darkness. Just the two of us and the sound of the sea. Not a star in the sky.

'Do you think we should have taken her to the doctor?' I said.

'She would never have gone.'

'There's a first aid place on the campsite. I checked before we booked.'

'She'll be all right. She's fine now.'

'She's still slurring her words.'

'Not like she was though. She'll be fine in the morning.'

'Well, let's keep an eye on her. We could try and take her out tomorrow. It looks like it might brighten up.'

'She'd like that. She hates noughts and crosses.'

'She's not the only one.'

'Have we got any paper left?'

'I think so.'

'You'd better get your ruler out. My hair's getting wet.'

Killing time

At four o'clock this afternoon, I'm taking Kipling to the vet. It's now half past six in the morning and he's asleep on the kitchen worktop. His back leg is half-hanging off the side. I don't know how he got there. He must have started sleep walking again. I reach past him, take the toaster from the cupboard and plug it in at the wall. It sparks blue when I push the lever down. I sit at the table and wait. The clock above the washing machine ticks and tocks. It sounds louder than normal. I watch the red finger go round. The black fingers stay perfectly still. I could watch them all day and never see them moving, even though I know that they are.

'Here comes breakfast, Kipling.'

I spread jam straight onto the toast and bite the first slice before I spread the second. There's another football in my back garden. It's getting light outside and I can see it through the window. I'll put it with the others under the stairs. Kipling belches in his sleep and for a second it looks like he might be waking up, but instead he snorts, breathes deeply and returns to his sleeping position. I finish my toast, put the plug in the sink and fill it with water and washing-up liquid. I wash my plate.

'We should be going walkies now.'

I sit back down at the table. There's a cobweb in the corner of the room above the door. A daddy long legs trapped and flailing around. I watch until it gives up.

'I think I'll go on my own, Kip. You don't mind, do you?'

I go upstairs, hang my pyjamas in the wardrobe and get dressed into my walking clothes. Trousers over long woollen socks, a shirt, tie and an old jacket my father gave me years ago. Its pockets are deep enough to hold a notepad. I go back downstairs, pull Kipling's lead from the key rack and throw it over my shoulder. I check on him before I leave the house. Surprise — he's still on the worktop. I know I should lift him down, but I don't want to wake him. He looks peaceful, almost healthy. So I open the front door. Step into the morning air.

★ ★ ★

I've lived in this town nearly all my life, since my parents moved into my grandmother's house when she died. I was two-years-old and the town was surrounded by enough fields to

130

fend off the slow creep of new housing. For years, it was a farming village, enclosed by rolling hills and fertile soil. But beneath the soil they found coal, tonnes of it, and Gutterton Half was just the start. The first in a long line of temporary scars on the landscape. Gradually, the place I grew up in has disappeared. When they've extracted all the coal, they restore the land, and always improve it. But it's never the same. Both above and below the surface.

I walk from Cressington Vale along the paths that wind through backs of houses and out to Tickle Brook, a narrow stream that circles the town and runs into a reservoir fifteen miles away. To get there, it must go through a pub. The Wethouse. It opened last year and will be closed by Christmas. The water flows straight through the middle and under a bridge, dissecting the bar. It was supposed to be a feature, something to attract people to the town, something to take pride in. The landlord had his picture in the paper two weeks running. The first with the ever-grinning mayor, cutting a ribbon and declaring the pub open. The second trying to explain the sanitary towels and used condoms that were floating past the punters.

Tickle Brook has a public footpath alongside it. This is the route I take with

Kipling when he's well enough. The dog mess bin is our turning point. It's in the corner of an almost-full cemetery. Behind it there's a small park. Just two swings and a seesaw covered in graffiti. Behind that is St Mary's Junior School. Forty kids to every teacher. Georgina worked there for twenty-five years. Until she had her first stroke. We used to walk to the dog mess bin together. Her with an armful of folders, me with my sandwich bags.

I walk quickly when Kipling's not with me. It's taken fewer than fifteen minutes and I'm already sat on the bench next to the bin. I take his lead from my pocket and twirl it like a lasso. Parents, mostly mothers, are getting their children to school. They kiss them goodbye and watch them through the school doors. The children collect in the playground before registration. The hedgerows are thin and I can see the playground swelling with bodies, hear it swelling with noise. I guess which one of them stitched the rocket into Judy's scarf. A group of boys are fighting beneath the weeping willows on the far side. One of them spits on the floor, pushes a girl with his elbow. I decide it was probably him.

An elderly woman comes through the gate and into the cemetery. She has a tight blue perm and a pit bull terrier. It squats casually, lifts its ribs and defecates next to a headstone.

Then it stands up, looks at her as if to say, 'There you go, sort that out'. The words engraved on the stone read, 'James 'Lucky Jim' McHoolie, 1899–1966, a wonderful granddad, father and son, in loving memory'. I wonder how many times it's had a dog line up next to it, ready to soil. The old woman reaches into her coat pocket and pulls out a pair of disposable gloves.

'Sandwich bags are cheaper,' I say.

'What?'

'I said it would be cheaper to use sandwich bags.'

'You'll have to speak up. I can't hear a word you're saying.'

'Sandwich bags.'

'Yes.'

'They're cheaper than disposable gloves.'

'Yes.'

'You should try them.'

'No, I don't think so, dear.'

'You'll save money in the long run.'

'No, I only need one pair. I'll run them under the tap when I get home.'

She puts her gloves on and picks up the pit bull faeces with two hands, cupped like she's drinking from a fountain. Then she opens the bin with her elbow, drops the faeces inside. Her dog comes to sit next to me on the bench. We watch her rip the gloves off her hands with her teeth. She bites them at the wrists, whips them away in one movement. Now inside out, she puts them back in her pocket and whistles to the dog. He trots proudly after her.

★ ★ ★

Ten minutes later, Mr Bowmer strides into the playground ringing a large brass bell. It makes an incredible sound. He only stops ringing when the last child is inside. He was assistant head for twenty-six years, during which he applied for the top job on three occasions, but never got it. On the last occasion they appointed Georgina. Fifteen years ago. We argued about it.

'Why aren't you happy for me?'

'I am happy for you.'

'You don't look like you are.'

'I am. You deserve it.'

'Work isn't everything,' she said. 'You can get whatever job you like.'

'Not really.'

'Yes you can. You're young enough. You should be happy for me. I've worked hard for this.'

'What's your job got to do with my job?'

'You're not happy.'

'I'm fine. Congratulations. Honestly.'

134

Mr Bowmer's hair is parted and plastered to his head and his trousers are two inches too short. Georgina detested him. She'd detest him even more if she knew he'd finally taken her job. They gave her a year to get well again after her first stroke. When she didn't make it, they said they had to look elsewhere. They said that they were sorry. It took another six months of interviews before they eventually appointed Bowmer. He started the job a fortnight ago. It was in the paper. I watch him prowl the empty schoolyard. He takes long slow steps, pausing every so often to look behind him. He walks past the outside toilets, a small terrapin building that's in need of replacing. There's a tap on one side for the children to drink from. He puts his hand in his jacket and pulls out a pair of pliers. I take out my notepad and pen.

Note: Time taken for it to stop dripping = 19 minutes and 11 seconds. Cut finger or thumb. Swears like Angelica. Sweats too much. Note end.

The cemetery also has a tap. It's attached to a piece of rotting wood that prevents its thin pipe from bending. People bring their jugs, beakers and empty washing up bottles to water their wreaths and flowers. The tap is being used by two men wearing identical jogging suits. I've seen them before, in the surgery waiting room. They are twins, around my age. I watch them fill their bottles with water, do a lap of the cemetery grounds then make their way out again. They both turn, hold up their hands and wave as they run past me. They take swigs from their bottles. All in perfect unison. Georgina and I had matching waterproof coats. We got them from a hiking shop on holiday. The 'Jacket in a Packet'. Buy one, get one free. They were black with a yellow stripe down the left arm. Don Donald had special 'his and hers' handkerchiefs made for him and his wife. He still wears 'his' in the pocket of his suit jacket. She took 'hers' with her when she left. John and Patricia Bonsall have the same fluorescent rubber suits. They wear them in the winter, to do the garden. I have all this on file, of course. Pages of it, under I for 'Identical clothing'.

I decide to walk the long way home and leave the cemetery via the south exit, which backs onto one of the new housing estates. Not that it's new anymore — they built it twenty years ago. Each street named after a type of tree or shrub. Oak Drive, Azalea Avenue, Chestnut Way. I walk for half a mile before the estate comes to an abrupt end, where the houses stop and the latest opencast coal site begins, a steep bank separating the two. It's only been here eighteen months. I stop and listen for the machines on the other side of the hill, deep in the ground. But I hear nothing, complete silence. Like there's nobody there.

It never used to be like this. There were no barriers around the site to stop you getting in, no noise monitors or acoustic fencing. Just a great, dirty hole in the ground, with even dirtier machines to make it wider and deeper. These days, the council agree specific sound levels with the environmental agency. There are rules and regulations in place. Back then we had a permanent growl that petered to a hum the further away you were from the nearest cut. These days, I may not hear the machines, but I can smell them. A faint whiff of dust and oil. It hangs in the air and scratches my throat. Most people don't notice, but I've lived here too long. I'm sensitised and cynical. I continue towards the centre of town, away from the site and nearer home. The smell disappears. It's replaced by car fumes and freshly-lit cigarettes. A queue outside Tesco. The building that transformed us from a village into a town. Like a cathedral in a city.

★ ★ ★

I turn into Cressington Vale. Benny is walking towards me. His limp looks worse than usual. It's quarter past nine in the morning. I had no idea. I'm usually home by now. Georgina will be waking up. I might have missed Angelica. I should have missed Benny, but he must be late for school. I want to stop him, talk to him. I want to tell him I've seen him painting with his eyes closed, that I know his secret. If he doesn't answer my questions, I'll tell everyone he's a fraud. I want to grab him by the scruff of the neck, hold him up against a tree and shout, 'Who do you think you are? You're just a boy.'

'Morning, Mr Kingdom,' he says, striding past in his stupid jacket with the childish badges attached to the lapel. They are all black. I can't read the writing.

'You're just a boy,' I reply, once he's out of earshot. He gets to the end of the street, turns around and looks at me. For a second, I think he's going to say something, but he just smiles, turns again and walks away. I look towards Angelica's house. The postman is knocking on her front door. I walk slowly down the street and into my garden. I face the house, look up at Georgina's window and pretend to search for my keys in my coat pocket. If Angelica opens her door, I can wander over and ask the postman if he has

138

any mail for me. The three of us can have a conversation. But he'll have to leave. He's got a job to do. I sneak a look over my shoulder. He's already left Angelica. He's moved next door and is shoving letters through the Martin's letterbox. He has no patience.

I step into the house and take off my coat. Georgina needs her tablets. She'll be wondering where I've been. There's a peculiar smell. Pork scratchings, burnt toast and diarrhoea. It's coming from the kitchen. I push the door open. The stench knocks me back. I have to hold my sleeve across my mouth and nose to stop me from gagging. There's a pile of dog mess on the floor beneath the worktop. It's splashed across the floor tiles and up the front of the cupboards. There is vomit on the draining board. I look at the wall, follow the lead from the plug in its socket to the toaster bobbing up and down in the sink. And then Kipling, with his head submerged and his eyes still open. Water and washing-up liquid. The tap dripping, like tears into an oil slick.

Kipling

'Hello? Yes, hello. I'd like to cancel an appointment. Yes. Yes. This afternoon. No, Kipling Kingdom. No. Well, I'm afraid it's rather too late for that. Yes. I'm absolutely positive. Thank you. Goodbye.'

'Sorted?'

'Yes, I think so.'

I give Don his phone back. Mine is still unplugged and Don thinks it's broken. He only bought his yesterday. It's cordless, which means he can stand twenty-five metres from the receiver and it'll still work. He's very pleased with it. We're about to bury Kipling. It's been two hours since I found him. I spent the first hour clearing up the mess in the kitchen and the second digging a hole in the front lawn. Don's wearing the suit he got married in. It's black velvet. For special occasions. I told him he didn't need to change, but he insisted. I'm still in my walking clothes. I've taped the hole in Kipling's box so his head won't hang out. I roll my shoulders and take a deep breath. Georgina is sleeping inside. Don thinks she's staying with my parents. He looked surprised

140

when I told him. The morning clouds are beginning to separate. Blue sky is appearing in patches. It looks like the sun might come out.

'Dog dead is it?' says a voice from the other side of the garden fence. It's Annie Carnaffan, our next door neighbour.

'Go away,' says Don. 'You're not welcome here.'

'I live here.'

'That doesn't mean you're welcome.'

I remember Annie Carnaffan's face the day Georgina arrived home from hospital in a converted minibus. They opened the back doors and lowered her wheelchair onto the road. A face at every window. One of the hospital staff started pushing her towards the house, but I stopped them. I wanted to push her. It was my job. I grabbed the handles and took over. Halfway down the path one of the wheels got caught on a crack in the concrete. The chair toppled over and Georgina began to fall. I couldn't take her weight. But Don was behind me and managed to grip the arm of the chair. He pulled it steady. I stopped, composed myself, shaking. Someone was watching me. Annie Carnaffan, grinning from behind her bedroom window, her face scrunched at the eyes, searching for misery. And I'll never forget it. I won't forgive her.

'Just get on with it,' she says. Don opens his mouth to say something back, but stops as Gerald Winnett-Smith, my other next door neighbour, slams his front door shut. We hear his wife, Bonnie, stamping upstairs, so Gerald knows she's not just angry, she's very angry. He tugs at his coat sleeves, nods in our direction and walks sheepishly down the street. I don't speak to the Winnett-Smiths either. Georgina overheard them talking during one of their barbecue 'gatherings'. We were in the garden. Georgina was reading and I was asleep. 'They've never had kids, you know. I hear Gordon fires blanks.' I remember waking up, desperately needing the toilet. Georgina was at the other end of the garden, her thumb on the end of the hosepipe, water spraying gently over the fence and onto Gerald's barbecue. 'Go back to sleep,' she mouthed as Bonnie started screaming. I winked at Georgina, smiled and gave her a double thumbs up.

Note: Winnett: a dried-up ball-like piece of excrement matted in the hairs between a person or animal's buttocks. Often called clegnut or dingleberry. Note end.

We've had two minutes of silence, which is one more than they give to important people

142

when they die. I'm trying to think of something to say, but can't. Don is fidgeting next to me. I can hear him rattling. Loose change in every pocket. It's stopping me from thinking straight. I want this over and done with. Kipling is dead. It's hitting me. I don't want to be here. I want to go inside and write something down. Sit behind a curtain. Bake a cake. I can hear Annie Carnaffan. She's still there, wheezing behind the hedge. Horrible little woman. We should be burying her. Stop rattling. I have nothing to say. This is Jonathan's fault. Stupid paedophile. Angelica is coming.

'Good morning,' she says, flicking the stub of her cigarette onto the pavement. 'Or should that be afternoon?'

'No, it's still morning,' Don replies. 'Just.'

'Oh well. What're you two up to?'

She can't see Kipling. I dug the hole next to the fence and she's on the other side. She's oblivious. Don's looking at me. He wants to know what I want him to say. I don't care what he says. I want to know if they've met before.

'Watching squirrels,' he says.

'Really? Where?'

'They've gone now. Two of them. One had a nut in its mouth. I think the other one was trying to steal it.'

'Where did they go?'

'They ran away. I think they were together. Like a couple.' Angelica stares at Don. He nods at her. Like he's never told a lie in his life.

'So Gordon, is Kipling any better?'

'Not really,' I say.

'Oh, I'm sorry. Do we know what's wrong with him yet?'

'He's dead.' She cups her mouth with her hands. I imagine the smell on her fingers. Stale smoke. She has mascara smudged across the bridge of her nose. She must've slept in it.

'That's awful. When?'

'This morning.'

'He electrocuted himself,' Don butts in.

'Oh my god, Gordon!'

He points at the box. Angelica leans over the fence, lets out a shriek and jumps backwards. She stands there, takes her hands from her mouth. I know what she's thinking.

'Did he do it on purpose?' she asks.

'I doubt it,' I say. 'He's a dog.'

'They throw themselves into quarries all the time,' says Don.

'Kipling doesn't,' I say, even though it doesn't make sense. This is ridiculous. The whole situation is ridiculous. I have to get this over with. What a way to go.

'Angelica, would you like to join us? We're about to bury him,' I say. She puts her hands under her armpits and folds her arms.

'No, I shouldn't. I hardly knew him.' She edges away, starts walking back across the road.

'Are you sure?' shouts Don.

'Yes, you two carry on.'

'Okay, see you later Angie.'

Angie? Angie? So, they do know each other. I don't believe it. Why would she be friends with Don? He's just a lonely old man. I've never seen them talking. Hold on. She's not shouting back. She's still walking away from us. Maybe they're not so familiar. Don's just pushing his luck, calling her Angie like that. She's opening the door. Going, going, gone. She doesn't remember his name. But she knows my name.

'Nice girl,' says Don.

'She's forty-two,' I reply.

'Really? She doesn't look it.'

'Dogs don't commit suicide,' says a voice from beyond the fence. 'They haven't got the sense.'

'I wish you had the sense, Annie,' says Don. He waits for a reply, but for the second time in the space of a minute, he doesn't get one. Instead, we hear the sound of heels scraping along concrete followed by the slam of a door.

'Let's get him buried,' I say, bending down and lifting one side of the box. I can feel the weight transfer as Kipling slides to the other end. He's incredibly heavy.

'Quick, grab it.'

Don lifts his end and immediately looks like he's about to keel over. His hands shake, the weight becomes too much and he has to let go. We drop it from a standing position. It hits the damp earth with an almighty thump. I imagine Kipling whimpering inside.

'Where's the spade?' says Don. 'You go and put your feet up. I'll fill him in.'

* * *

Thirty seconds later. I'm behind the curtain watching Don to see if he steals my spade. He drags the soil into the hole with the back of the blade. It takes him seven minutes. When he's finished, he gets on his knees and levels the soil with the palms of his hands. Then he puts them together and bows his head. It looks like he's praying. A minute later he arches his neck to the sky and crosses himself. He gets it wrong, does it back to front. As he stands up and walks away, a squirrel jumps over the fence and buries a nut in Kipling's grave. He's not even cold. Don doesn't notice. He's busy crossing the road with my spade under his arm, wiping tears from his cheeks with his sleeves. I thought he might get upset, but I knew he'd want to help. That's why I asked him. And I couldn't lift the box on my own.

'Does Georgina know?' he'd said when I knocked on his door and broke the news.

'No not yet.'

'Is she still at your mum and dad's?'

'Yes.'

'Do you want to use the phone?'

'No. I'll tell her when she gets back. She'll only get upset.'

'You're right. Probably for the best.'

★ ★ ★

Angelica has returned. She's leaving her house, closing her door and walking towards Don. She shouts something to him. He stops and gives his eyes a final wipe. Then he leans on my spade like nothing's happened. He's fine. Just got something in his eye. Both eyes. She reaches out and puts her hand on his shoulder, tips her head to one side. She's feigning sympathy. She doesn't care. They hardly know each other. Don's shaking his head and smiling. He's fine, absolutely fine. He holds the spade like a cane and tries to jump and click his heels in the air. He gets three inches off the ground and twists his ankle when he lands. Angelica's got her arm around his shoulder. There's nothing wrong with him. He's nodding his head and hobbling away. They're saying goodbye. She smiles. He waves and limps. She wanders off down the street and into the distance, her arms folded as always. Her small steps.

I've been here fifteen minutes. I want a cup of tea and a piece of sponge cake. I need to check on Georgina. I can still smell Kipling's diarrhoea. I told her it was me, that I'd only just made the toilet. It must have been those vegetables. I told her to rest, go back to sleep and that I'd check on her later. Then I closed the door and used my coat to block the gap at the bottom where the smell could get through. Kipling's lead fell out of the pocket. Now it's starting to rain and I can hear the floorboards creaking above me. Georgina must be waking. I want to wait for Angelica. I want to see if I can work out where she's been. But I need to be upstairs. I need to drag my wife to her commode. Help her through the process. I need to lie and tell her that Kipling's staying at Don's tonight.

Ladders

Don helped me and Georgina decorate. We worked every weekend for six months and sometimes in the evenings after work. We finished the final room the week before we went on our honeymoon. My father came to join us for the last push. He arrived in a blue van with three ladders attached to its roof, each one a different size. He'd borrowed it from someone at work. A mate of his who owed him one. I was painting the windowsill in the bedroom when he pulled up outside our house. Georgina heard it from the bathroom. She came in to find out what the noise was. She stood behind me and put her hands on my shoulders. We watched him reverse up and onto the pavement. He turned the engine off, looked in the rear view mirror and ran his hands through his hair. I smiled as he stepped out of the van and looked up at the window. The three of us waved together. My father was wearing the clothes he wore for work. A pair of jeans and a plain white, long-sleeved shirt rolled up to the elbows. That's what he always wore. If either garment developed a hole my mother would sew it up.

When the hole came back she would do it again. If it became unsewable, she would buy him near-identical replacements. Jeans and rolled up shirt sleeves. My father's work clothes. Soaked in coal dust and cigarette smoke. Grimy to touch and forever familiar.

'Here I am,' he shouted as he entered the house. 'How are the workers?' I placed my paintbrush on the rim of the tin and met him at the foot of the stairs. Georgina went back to work.

'We've nearly finished.'

'Fantastic. I've brought some ladders.'

'Yes, we saw.'

'They came with the van.'

'Morning Arthur,' Georgina shouted from the bathroom. 'Thanks for coming.'

'Morning love. Not a problem. Come and get the kettle on. Tell me what's what.'

'Get the kettle on yourself. No sugar for me. Gordon can bring it back up.'

My father looked at me, smiled and shook his head. 'Is she always like this?' he said.

'More or less,' I replied.

'Well you'd better get used to it. There's no turning back now. Go and put the kettle on. Two sugars.'

I walked to the kitchen and knocked on the window. Don was outside in the garden. I held an imaginary mug to my mouth and mimed. He gave me thumbs up and got back to work. He was making a rockery out of stones he'd found at Gutterton Half. They'd been piled up by the worker's entrance. A crowd had started to gather. People were helping themselves. Don raced back to Cressington Vale and told me what he'd seen. We went back with two pillowcases and a wheelbarrow. By the time we arrived the stones were almost gone, but we took what we could.

'Who's that in the garden?' said my father.

'It's Don Donald. He lives across the road.'

'The one whose wife went?'

'That's him.'

'How's he bearing up?'

'Not well. He's keeping busy.'

'By doing your garden?'

'He's been a great help.'

'I'll bet he has. Every cloud, eh?'

'I suppose so.'

My father paused, sighed and scratched his chin. 'I don't know what he's worried about. How old is he? Twenty-five? He'll find someone else.'

I switched the kettle on at the wall and arranged four mugs on the worktop. My father watched Don in the garden. He tapped the floor with his toecaps. Drummed the sink with fingers. 'I'll have a word with him,' he said.

151

We sat outside and drank our tea together. My father and me on the doorstep and Don perched on the upturned wheelbarrow. Georgina came to join us, her overalls covered in paint-coloured finger marks. She sipped her tea and surveyed the half-finished rockery. Don watched her and waited anxiously. He looked at us and raised his eyebrows. Georgina turned and nodded at him. 'Looks great,' she said. 'You're doing a grand job.' Don smiled and nodded back. Georgina sat behind him on the wheelbarrow, so they were back-to-back. Our break lasted forty minutes. We listened to my father tell stories between cigarettes. All from work and all second hand apart from the last, which was about my mother's hysterectomy. He had Don in stitches.

After our second round of tea we went back to work. Georgina in the bathroom and me at my windowsill. We left my father outside with Don and the rockery. They worked all afternoon and into the evening. My father used one of his ladders and an old skirting board to make a ramp for the wheelbarrow. He carried the stones from one side of the garden to the other and Don placed them carefully into position. Both of

152

them bare-chested. One with a broken heart, the other pushing fifty. I could hear them laughing from the bedroom. It reminded me of when Georgina and me were younger, listening to our parents after dinner. Getting drunk and having fun without us.

My father came in when the light started to fade. He put his shirt back on, made himself another cup of tea and joined us upstairs. Georgina was with me in the bedroom. I'd spent the previous hour trying to attach a shelf to the wall. She thought that it was straight, but I knew it wasn't.

'Right, I'm off when I've had this drink. Don's still outside. I told him to leave it for the night, but he wouldn't listen. He's nearly finished.'

'Thanks, Dad. He'll be all right.' My father entered the room and stood next to us. We were in a line. He twisted his neck, bent his knees and stared at the shelf from across the room. Then he straightened, scratched his chin and repeated the process.

'That's not straight,' he said.

'I knew it! I told you it wasn't straight.' Georgina put her hands to her cheeks in disbelief and started walking to the door. 'I told you,' I said. 'I knew it wasn't straight.'

'Do what you like with it, Gordon,' she replied. 'It's only a shelf.' I took my screwdriver from my tool belt and walked over to the shelf. I turned to my father and winked at him.

'Not that side,' he said.

'What?'

'Not that side. It needs going left a bit.'

'Left a bit? You mean right a bit.'

'No I mean left a bit. Come and look.'

'I don't need to look. Are you serious?'

'Of course I'm serious. It's not straight.'

'I know it's not straight. I've been saying it's not straight for over an hour.'

'Give me the screwdriver.'

'No.'

'Come on, give me the screwdriver. Let me do it.' My father put his tea on the windowsill and held out his hand.

'I painted that this morning. Is it dry?'

'It's fine. Give it me.' He walked towards me and tried to snatch the screwdriver from my hand. I moved quickly and hid it behind my back. He paused, and before I could react, he jabbed me in the ribs with his index and middle fingers together. It didn't hurt, but it was enough to throw me off guard. I turned my back on him instinctively. He grabbed my wrist with one hand and took the screwdriver with the other. All in one movement. I decided not to argue any further. I walked to the other side of the room and let him get on with it. It took him nearly half an hour to take the shelf apart and screw it back to the wall. Exactly where he wanted. I watched, waited and drank his tea while he did it. Just to get my own back.

★ ★ ★

It was late by the time my father left. Don walked with him to the van and helped him re-attach the ladder to the roof. They shook hands and laughed. When they stopped laughing, my father put his hand on Don's arm, leant towards him and whispered something. Then they laughed again. My father opened the van door and climbed inside. Don tapped the bonnet with the palm of his hand and walked home. I stood on my doorstep and waved. By the time I'd washed up, locked the back door and made my way upstairs, Georgina was in bed with the light switched off. I changed into my pyjamas and went to the bathroom. It smelled of paint and detergent. I held my breath while I cleaned my teeth, inhaling only once. We were nearly there. Our own house. Our own furniture. Fully decorated. I climbed into bed with Georgina.

'Are you asleep?' I said, softly. She didn't answer. I reached beneath the covers and put my hand on her hip. 'Georgie, are you asleep?'

'Not any more,' she mumbled.

'Sorry. Are you okay?'

'I'm fine. Have they gone?'

'About twenty minutes ago. I've cleared up downstairs. The paint still smells.'

'That's paint for you,' she said, rolling over and away from me, my fingers sliding around her waist as she turned. I removed my hand and adjusted the pillows. I lay with my eyes open. They adjusted quickly to the dark. I was able to trace the outline of the moon through the curtains. I listened to Georgina's breathing. It hadn't changed. It hadn't slowed.

'Georgie?' I whispered. She sighed and tugged the covers.

'What now, Gordon?'

'I've just been thinking, that's all.'

'About what?'

'Nothing really. Just the wedding.'

'What about it?'

'I don't know. I've just been thinking.'

'It's late, Gordon. Go to sleep.' Georgina shuffled on her elbows. Changed position. Sighed again.

'You remember on the way home, when we dropped your mum off, she left her earrings in the car?'

'She was drunk.'

'Completely. Do you remember?'

'Sort of. Not really.'

'My dad helped her into the house and I went in after them. I took your mum her earrings. They were hugging.' Georgina didn't answer straight away. She thought about her reply. I turned onto my side. I put my hand on her hip.

'So what?' she said. 'What's your point?'

'I don't have a point.'

'Then why bring it up?'

'I've just been thinking about the wedding. I thought it was strange.'

'You need to stop thinking, Gordon; Go to sleep.' She lifted one of her pillows and placed it over her head, clamped it with her forearm. I lay a little longer, my eyes open, staring at the moon.

'I'm going to straighten the shelf in the morning,' I said. Georgina didn't reply.

Misconduct

Two days have passed since we buried
Kipling. The smell of diarrhoea has disappeared and Don Donald still has my spade.
It's five to nine in the morning and Benny is
late for school. I've been watching his front
door for half an hour and he's yet to emerge.
Last night I saw him painting, so I know that
he's not ill. I sat on the edge of the bed and
let my mind wander. I thought about what it
was like when I used to wake up in the
morning, put on a shirt and go to work. What
it was like to have two incomes and no cause
for help. How it felt to go to church at the
weekend with faith and no questions. I
watched Benny's candles melt in the
half-light. One of them needs replacing. It's
almost down to nothing.

Angelica's door opens. She steps out and
into the morning, turns and locks her door.
Her hair is half up, half down. It looks like it's
been trimmed. She's carrying an umbrella
and wearing the jeans she wore the day she
moved to Cressington Vale. The ones with the
colours sewn into the hem. She holds her
palm flat and feels for rain. Then she looks at

the sky and holds her hand out further. There is no rain. It stopped more than an hour ago. Angelica turns around, slides the tip of her umbrella into the letterbox and shoves the rest of it through by the handle. I write it down and watch her walk to the pavement. She flicks her hair and pulls her coat tight around her waist. She's on her way to the newsagents. I'll make a fresh cup of tea while she's gone.

I put down my notepad and pen, push myself up with my elbows and make my way to the kitchen. Before I leave the room, I turn and take one last look through the window. Angelica has stopped. She's standing at the end of Benny's drive and opening the gate. She's walking towards the house and knocking on the door. I go back to the curtain and pick up my pen. I look at my watch and make a note of the time.

Note: Angelica is 42 and Benny is 16. He is younger than the distance between them. Average age of menopause onset = 51. Note end.

Angelica has been inside Benny's house for seven minutes. His mother left for work while I ate my breakfast, which means that no-one else is home. Just Benny and Angelica. My fingers are shaking. My heart is racing. It's completely inappropriate. Whatever they're doing. She knocked three times before he answered the door. He opened it slowly, smiled at her and yawned. I could see the hair in his armpits. Angelica spoke to him. Benny shook his head. She spoke again and made a shape with her hands. This time he nodded. He took a step backwards and beckoned her inside. She looked around, searched the street for faces and followed him into the house.

Nine minutes and counting. I'm still waiting for Angelica to reappear and doing everything I can to stop myself from going over there to interrupt. I want to ask her what the hell she thinks she's doing. I want to ask her if she knows what it looks like to the rest of us. But I don't need to interrupt, because Angelica is opening the door and leaving the house. Her arms are wrapped tight around her chest and she looks angry. As angry as she did when I first saw her at the surgery. She has something in her hand, but I can't tell what it is because it's too small and she's moving so quickly. Benny appears in the doorway. He looks even angrier. His face is red and his fists are jabbing the air. He shouts at Angelica, but she ignores him. She bows her head, continues through the gate and away down the street.

When she reaches the end she stops, turns and looks back at Benny. He looks at her. They stand thirty metres apart but hold each other's stare for what seems like an eternity. Until one of them cracks. Angelica. She touches her forehead, looks down at the ground and shrugs her shoulders. She covers her eyes with her hand and walks away from Cressington Vale. Benny steps into the house and pumps his fist in celebration. He smiles and slams the door.

I make notes for the next twenty minutes. I've never seen anything like it.

Morale

Georgina knows that Kipling is dead. She worked it out when I told her he was staying with Don for the third night running. She didn't believe me. We'd been playing noughts and crosses. She drew lines and circles on the paper with her finger. I copied her instructions with the pen. She beat me fair and square.

When we'd finished she put her hand on my arm, pointed to the dog hairs on my cardigan. She took my hand, squeezed it once. 'He's still with Don,' I said, without looking at her. I took my hand away, shuffled the papers on the bed and tried to look sincere. Georgina started crying. It was the first time she'd cried since the night she had her second stroke. And she couldn't stop. The tears poured from her eyes. I sat with her, wiped them away with tissues and toilet roll. I put my arm around her shoulders, told her he was old and it was probably for the best. He's with the Lord now. But it made no difference. She continued to cry. Then after more than an hour, she fell asleep. I waited until I knew she wouldn't wake up. Arranged her pillows and put her in position. I sat in the chair by the bed. My back ached from sitting on the mattress. It ached even more on the chair. But I had to stay with Georgina. One eye had stopped, but the other continued to weep while she slept.

Note: Expect dry eyes and reduced lid control leading to poor closure. Tears do not necessarily relate to levels of discomfort. Note end.

I collected every item of clothing in the house. From underpants to overcoats. Georgina's and mine. I folded them up and put them into piles in the spare room. Then I went to Wilkinson, bought every roll of Sellotape they had. When I got home, I took the ironing board upstairs, opened it by the spare room window. I watched John Bonsall. He must have had the day off work to finish his conservatory. Every twenty minutes he appeared at his front door. He was wearing his fluorescent rubber suit. It used to fit him. He sipped from his mug, stood for a while and sucked in the cold winter air. Then he disappeared again, went back to his 'work'.

I cut off strips of Sellotape. Hundreds of them. I used them to remove every trace of Kipling I could find. I put each item of clothing on the ironing board, dragged the tape across the fabric. When I finished, I started on the furniture, beginning with Georgina's bed, making sure I didn't wake her. It took me four and a half hours to complete the house. It had gone dark outside. I sat by the spare room window, sweat dripping from my forehead onto the sill. Pamela Bonsall pulled into the drive. John was standing by the door, waiting for her. He had his mug in his hand and a smile on his face. He kissed her on the cheek, pretended to wipe sweat from his brow. I picked up a notepad and pen, and began to write.

★ ★ ★

I think Georgina may be deteriorating. I'm beginning to doubt my capability. This morning, I tried to get her to stand up. We've been practicing. Last week, she managed to stand for thirty seconds. She even took a step. But this morning she refused to even try. Her skin was pale and she barely touched her breakfast. She struggled to drink her water and take her tablets. I told her not to worry. I told her we'd have another go later if she wanted. But she looked at me as if to say, 'No, not today.' And I sat there, watched her staring at nothing. Or at our wedding picture

164

on the dresser. At the mirror above it, too high for her to see a reflection of herself. Just the window by her side, the thick curtains and the strip of sky where they fail to meet. She looked terrified and angry. I picked up the manual, licked my thumb and flicked through the pages. For the first time in weeks, I didn't know what to do. There was nothing I could do. I closed the manual and put it back on the bedside table. I sat and I stared. I watched Georgina's eyes close. She looked older than she ever has before. She looked like her mother.

'What if I can't do this?' I whispered, but Georgina was already asleep, her mouth slightly open, the smallest gap for her to breathe through. I put my hand on her forehead and checked her temperature. 'Don would help if I asked him. He always wants to help.'

Nobody's business

It's quarter past three in the afternoon and I've spent the last two days thinking about Benny and Angelica's argument. Thirty seconds ago I was upstairs in the bedroom. I'd opened the window so that I could hear the street in case something happened. Instead, I heard Don whistling his way into my front garden. I had to run downstairs and block him off, before he got to the door. He's in his suit again.

'Did you hear the commotion then?'

'Morning Don. What commotion was that?'

'Jenny's lad. Shouting his mouth off at the new girl.'

'You mean Angelica?'

'That's the one. Right here in the street.'

'She's not really a girl.'

'Well you know what I mean.'

'No I didn't see anything.'

'Me neither, but I heard them. Well, I heard him anyway.' Don laughs and snorts without meaning to. He half-wipes his nose with his sleeve. I turn and check I've closed the door correctly.

'What were they arguing about?' I say.

'I've got no idea. It was mainly him. He was effing and blinding. She said she didn't want to talk about it. He's a strange one.'

'You spoke to Angelica? When did you speak to her?'

'She was at the surgery when I picked up my prescription.'

'At the surgery? What was she doing there?'

'I don't know. I didn't ask. She looks like Christine, don't you think?'

'Christine? No. Not at all.'

'Not even a bit?'

'Not in the slightest. The last time you saw Christine she was twenty-one. That was over thirty years ago. You don't know what she looks like now.'

'No, but if she'd stayed.'

'But she didn't. They have different coloured hair. What did Angelica say about Benny?'

'She didn't say anything.'

'Nothing at all?'

'No, nothing. I mentioned it to her and she told me that she didn't want to talk about it. I didn't want to pry.'

'That's it? You should have pushed her. Neighbourhood security.'

'Well I didn't. So there you go.'

I'm making Don feel uncomfortable. This

would be an ideal time to tell him about Georgina. I could invite him in for a cup of tea and a piece of cake. I could explain to him what's happening. I think about our evenings in together when Georgina was recovering. Our Tuesdays and Thursdays. Everything he did for me. If I can persuade him not to tell anyone, we can help her to get well again. Like we did the last time. I look at Don and the unwiped mucus on his upper lip. He's combed his hair into a side parting.

'Why are you wearing the suit?' I ask. Don's expression changes. That's all he was after. A change of subject. Nothing awkward.

'Eric Devaney. We buried him this morning.'

'Who?'

'Eric. He used to work with your dad.'

'That doesn't help. I don't recognise the name. How did you know him?'

'Just from seeing each other.'

'Where?'

'Round and about. Shopping. Just round and about.'

'And you went to the funeral?'

'Yes, his wife invited me.'

'You didn't tell me about it.'

'You don't even know him.'

'Neither did you by the sounds of it.'

Don tries to reply but cannot find the

words. He almost looks upset. I want to speak to him about Georgina, but instead I'm bringing tears to his eyes. This hasn't happened for months.

'Have you come for your pickled onions?'

'No, not really. I came to say hello. That's all. See how you were.'

'I'm fine.'

'How did Georgina take the news?'

'What news?'

'About Kipling.'

'Right, I see.'

'Is she still at your parents? What's she doing there?'

'Helping them decorate.'

'Really? That's good news. What did she say about Kipling? Was she upset? I've been upset. I bet she was, wasn't she?'

The tears have disappeared and Don is now on the offensive. This is what he does. He tries to help but he wants to know too much. He's unreliable. If I tell him anything, he'll share it with the world. He's a gossip. A nosy neighbour. I need to end this conversation, before he invites himself in.

'Don, this really isn't your business,' I say. 'Not anymore.'

He opens his mouth to reply but once again the words don't arrive. He doesn't know what to say to me. The tears return and settle in the corners of his eyes. He does his best to keep them there, to stop them dribbling down his cheeks. I didn't want this to happen. It didn't need to be this way. Don turns and walks away from me. He gets to the end of the garden, stops and looks back.

'What's your problem, Gordon? What's wrong with you? She's better now. There are no excuses. I'm telling you. I won't have it. Not again.'

He doesn't wait for a response and I don't offer one. Instead I watch him cross the road, muttering under his breath. It takes him more than forty seconds. I wait until he's gone. Then I open the door, go back inside to Georgina.

Note: Angelica has been to the surgery three times in as many weeks. Repeat prescription possible. Something serious? Note end.

It's been four hours and fifteen minutes since I spoke to Don. I've been thinking about our conversation and I've decided I should speak to him again and ask him to return my spade. Three weeks ago, I had to steal back my clippers. I'm not going to steal back my spade. Instead, I'm going to ask for it politely. Georgina has been fed and watered. That's what she calls it. Fed and watered, like a plant or a flower. I'm standing in the middle of Cressington Vale. The street is empty. No cars, no neighbours, no strangers. The moon is barely visible, just a sliver of white on black. I stare at it, two rows of houses either side of me. I look back at the landing light that creeps into Georgina's bedroom. It's dim through the curtains. You can barely tell that it's there.

I walk past Don's wheelie bin, up and into his drive. The house is in darkness, because he never switches the lights on in the front. He only ever sits in the kitchen, which is round the back. Even when you knock on his door, like I am now, the lights stay off. He'd rather walk in the dark than pay for the electricity. You can hear him coming. Loose change rattling. I'm listening for it. He's going to open the door in his pyjamas. I wait thirty seconds. He probably didn't hear me. I knock again, a little harder. Sometimes he whistles. It becomes louder the nearer he gets. He has three songs, all of which he made up himself. I know them note for note. I press my ear to the door. Still no answer.

I walk down the path by the side of his house. It's overgrown with weeds that sprout up through the cracks in the slabs. There's a patch of different-coloured concrete where the wheelie bin lives. I step over it and into the back garden. I look up at the house. The rooms at the back are dark as well. I walk to the fence, lean back to try and see a light through the bedroom, but there isn't one. Don's compost heap is now gigantic. I think about climbing up the side to get a better view. Then I notice that the shed door is slightly ajar. A shred of light flickering through the cracked window. I look closer. It's a candle dancing, like Benny's candles dance.

I walk slowly across the grass and stand by the door of the shed. I look in through the gap by the frame. There are candles all over the floor and less than half of them are lit. The rest have either disappeared or gone out. I push on the door with my foot. It opens slowly, and there's Don Donald, my best friend, sat dead on his chair in his black velvet suit, arm across his chest, underpants around his ankles. Skidmarked from front to back. On his desk is a picture. A young blonde woman with a loose perm and a hole through her forehead. Christine. His wife that was. I walk slowly towards him and pick up my spade by the window. It has a post-it note attached to the handle. It says, 'Sorry about this morning, didn't mean to pry.' I pull up his underpants, zip his trousers and buckle his belt. I take the picture from the desk and re-attach it to the dartboard. The same dart through the same hole. Before I leave, I blow out the candles. Then I pick them up, take them outside and hide them in the compost.

He'd have done the same for me.

New testament

Don's funeral is tomorrow. I'm standing outside the church gates and looking up at the clock that hasn't worked for years. This is the first time I've been here since Judy broke into my house. She's inside preparing for Sunday Mass. I was hiding behind one of the trees on the opposite side of the road when her car arrived. It has a black sticker with white writing stuck to the inside of the rear window. It reads, 'Trust me, I'm a vicar.' I watched Judy climb out of the car, reach into the air, stretch and yawn. She walked to the boot and pulled out a leather briefcase. It was black and had her initials written on the side with Tipp-Ex. She also took out a red and transparent striped plastic bag with a pair of shoes inside. And what looked like a banana. Judy closed the boot, made her way through the graves and stopped at the church door. It took her three attempts to find the right key. I stayed out of view the entire time.

★ ★ ★

I've come to church because I want to speak to Judy about what has happened. I want her to tell me that everything will be okay. That's what she's paid for and that's what she does best. I've been expecting her to visit us again. She knows that I've been missing Mass and I thought she might want to know where I've been. There is rain in the air. My fingers are wrapped around the cold metal of the church gates. I take two steps forwards and then stop. I need to know what I'm going to say when I get inside. I have to have a plan of action. How will I start the conversation? With Kipling? Don? Georgina? Angelica perhaps. How much does a reverend really need to know?

This is exactly how I felt a year ago. The first and only other time I've spoken to Judy about a problem. She was new then and Georgina had made little progress in the six months since her stroke, so I decided to stay behind after Sunday service. It was a beautiful day. Glorious sunshine. Judy told us about a fifty-year-old woman who lived in her previous parish and had started running marathons when she found out her father was dying of cancer. A fortnight before he died, her father ran one with her. He did it in his wheelchair. She pushed him all the way. I waited until the service had finished and Judy was saying her goodbyes. I stood at the end of the queue. When she got to me, she shook my hand and smiled.

'Last one out today?'

'Yes, it looks like it.' She tried to let go of my hand but I held on tight and watched her smile disappear. She knew what was coming. It happened all the time. She was trained for this kind of thing. 'Could you spare me five minutes?'

'Of course, Gordon,' she said. 'Would you like a cup of tea?'

'Thank you. Yes please.'

I followed Judy through the door at the back of the church and into a small room with a sink, one chair and a microwave. I'd been in there before, but it looked different. Judy had decorated.

'This is my new kitchen,' she said. 'Sit yourself down. How can I help?'

The chair was smaller than a normal-sized chair because she'd made it herself at night class and only had a certain amount of wood. One of the legs was shorter than the others, which meant it rocked from side to side when I sat on it. I watched Judy fill the kettle with water from the tap. She was waiting for me to ask her my question. Standing over me. Like an angel or a skyscraper.

'How do you keep faith?' I said. Judy

176

turned off the tap.

'That's an interesting question. Do you mean how do I keep faith or how does anyone keep faith at all?'

'The second one. When it's hardest to believe.'

Judy paused. She looked away from me, opened the microwave and took out two china teacups and two teabags. She placed them on the worktop.

'The microwave is also the cupboard,' she said. I tried to look impressed. Judy plugged the kettle in at the wall and flicked the switch. She wiped her hands on her gown and turned slowly. She bent her knees and knelt on the floor. We were equal heights again. 'Gordon, you've had quite a shock to the system. There's no shame in admitting that things have been terribly tough. And it's at times like this, when things are at their toughest, that you need your faith the most. The Lord is with you. Make no mistake about it. And your family too, I'm sure.'

'There is no family. We have no children.'

'No. What about your parents? Your brothers and sisters?'

'I was an only child and so was Georgina. Both her parents are dead.'

'Well, I'm sorry to hear that. Your own

mother and father? They must be a source of support.'

'I haven't seen them since Georgina had her stroke. Six months ago.'

'Goodness me, Gordon. Why ever not?'

'Because my father blames me for what happened. He thinks that it was my fault.'

'It was no-one's fault, Gordon. Are you sure that there hasn't been a misunderstanding?'

'I'm positive. He told me a week after the stroke when we were at the hospital. My mother left the room to get some fresh air and my father sat on the edge of the bed. He said he'd always liked Georgina. That she was part of the family. But she wasn't a believer. Not like the rest of us.'

'But he didn't say that it was your fault.'

'No. But that's what he meant. That she was being punished. And that I should have seen it coming. Asked her to change.'

'What did you do?'

'I told him to leave. We haven't spoken since.'

Judy stood up, leaned on the sink and waited for the kettle to boil. She poured two cups of tea. I held mine with both hands and let the heat warm my fingers.

'Your faith, Gordon, is yours alone. Make of it what you will. It's not for me to tell you how to keep it. Your father neither. But I believe the Lord is with you.'

'How do you know?'

'I don't. It's just what I believe.'

★ ★ ★

It's now half past ten and I am walking home from church having not gone inside and having not spoken to Judy. The rain that was in the air before is now falling to the pavement, the houses and the cars driving past me. It's spitting in my face and rolling down my cheeks. This is the correct decision. This is the path I need to take. There is nothing that Judy can say or do to make things any better. What's done is done. I need to do things my way.

Non-attendance

It's the day of Don Donald's funeral and I'm standing on the central reservation of the dual carriageway. It connects the motorway to the town and there's supposed to be a service station on the junction. Hundreds of vehicles turn off every day. They get to the roundabout, find the service station is just a garage with 'coal scum' spray painted on the side and take the first exit back to the motorway. They're expecting toilets, treats and Burger King. They get petrol, pies and charcoal. And if it's summer, and they're lucky, they get bird tables.

I've already crossed the road heading into town. When the traffic breaks, I'll cross the road heading out. Cars are flashing past me: lorries, vans and motorbikes. They're an arm's length away. I lean back and grip the metal barrier. In the distance, a bus pulls into the fast lane to overtake a caravan. 200 yards away. 100 yards. 50 yards. I close my eyes and feel the gathering roar, the warm, fuel-filled air pressed against my face and the silence of my heart stopping for a moment. Then I open my eyes. The road is clear and it's safe to move. I make my way across the road, but have to stop in the slow lane, wait for a cyclist to pass.

Once I reach the other side, I start to walk along the hard shoulder. I put my fist to my mouth like a horn and whistle one of Don's songs. But I can't hear it. The sound is lost in the noise from the road. I can smell petrol fumes and cinnamon. The cinnamon is on my fingers from baking this morning. The petrol fumes are everywhere. I look around at the road, the clouds and the sky. Three glorious shades of grey. The police helicopter circling above me. Bright yellow metal, like a substitute sun. I pull my suit sleeve up and look at my watch. Don's funeral started thirty minutes ago. I keep whistling, march onwards to the garage for cigarettes. And a pornographic newspaper.

Note: The lorry game. 1 yellow. 2 blue. 3 green. 4 red (two Post Office). 6 plain metal black or grey. Note end.

'Hello, how are you?' says the assistant from behind the counter. He's new. He must be in his late twenties, which means he shouldn't be working in a garage. I've only just walked in. There's no need for him to speak to me yet.

'I'm just browsing,' I reply, even though it's a lie. I know exactly what I'm here for. But now I've said it, so I pretend to look at crisp packets, like I'm choosing between flavours. I pick up a carton of milk. Read the label. Put it back again.

'Let me know if you need any help.'

'Will do,' I say, and turn my back on him. I walk around the shop to the gift section. That's new as well. It contains pens with furry creatures shoved on the end. Road maps two years out of date. A big bag of bird seed with a sparkling gold star attached to the front. It reads, 'Half Prise' instead of price. Most of the display is taken up by travel games. They're on sale at 99p each. They take up two thirds of allotted 'gift' space. I assume they fell off the back of a lorry. I pick up Travel Scrabble and find Travel Magic Set underneath. I pick that up too and read the back of the box, which tells me it contains three dice, three plastic cups, a small sponge 'wonderball' and a red handkerchief. It also reads, 'Caution: Travel Magic not suitable for bumpy journeys and children under three years of age.'

'You can buy them both for £1.50,' says the assistant. 'It's a special offer.'

'Do you have any cigarettes?' I ask him as I

182

go to the counter. I look down at the badge pinned to his chest. His name is Martin and his cheeks are covered in pockmarks. They make him look ten years older than he probably is. 'How old are you?' I say.

'Eighteen,' he replies. He could pass for thirty.

'How long have you worked here?'

'Three days.'

'How much would fifteen litres of diesel cost me?'

'Are you getting petrol?'

'No, I said diesel.'

'It's just you don't have a car with you.'

'No, I *don't* have a car with me.'

'Is it parked round the side? I didn't see you pull in.'

'I don't have a car. I was testing you.'

'What was the test?'

'Fifteen litres of diesel.'

'What do you mean?'

'How much would it cost me to buy fifteen litres of diesel?'

'You don't have a car.'

'Forget it. I'd like to buy a packet of cigarettes.'

'What sort would you like?'

'What sort have you got?'

'We've got all sorts. You can get these — they're quite strong. Or these — they're like a low fat version. What do you normally smoke?'

'I don't normally smoke.'

'Then why do you want them?'

'I'm buying them for a friend. I'll take the strong ones.'

'Is he sixteen?'

'What do you mean?'

'Is your friend sixteen?'

'She's just turned forty-two.'

'That's fine. They told me I had to ask. We've had men coming in to buy fags for kids. I thought your friend might be underage.'

'We share the same birthday.'

'Are you going to buy the Travel Scrabble and the magic set?'

'I might do.'

'I kind of need to know.'

'Yes then. I'll buy them.'

'Anything else?'

'I'd like a newspaper please.'

'Which newspaper?'

'Do any have pornography inside?'

'What about this one?'

'What's it like?'

'Just tits and stuff.'

'That's fine.'

He turns around and starts pressing buttons on the till behind him. His uniform is too tight. His t-shirt rides up above his belt. I can see the hairs on the small of his back and a line of bumps where his spine moulds the skin. He has a scar the length of his forearm, elbow to wrist. It looks like the seam on an old-fashioned rugby ball. He holds his hand out and tells me how much I owe him. I place the exact change on the counter, coin by coin. He watches me do it, and then sighs when he has to pick them up. I collect my things and walk towards the door.

'You need to learn your petrol prices,' I tell him.

★ ★ ★

Outside it's started raining. The clouds have burst and I can't look up at the sky because the water's coming down so hard. I wish I'd put my coat on. Instead, I'm wearing my funeral suit. My white shirt has come untucked at the waist. It's wet through. I can see my nipples. The police helicopter has disappeared in the rain, but I can hear it whirling up above, hovering over the dual carriageway. It's four o'clock and starting to get dark. The traffic feels much closer than it did before, so I leave the hard shoulder and scramble halfway up the embankment. I can see a shower of red in the distance. Brake lights creeping towards me. A queue forming. It's probably an accident. Someone driving too fast. They've lost control and piled into a tree or another vehicle. I can see the helicopter again. Two beams in the sky dissecting each other, looking for trouble. Now they've stopped. They've fixed themselves in position. They shine down on where the accident must have happened. To where the queue begins. But I can't hear sirens. All I hear is the rain drumming against my shoulder pads and car engines aching to a grumble. I try to walk quicker so I can get closer, faster. But I slip and fall on one knee. It leaves a patch of mud on my trousers.

Ten minutes later. The queue is now huge. It will soon be on the motorway and in tomorrow's newspaper. I try and get to the top of the embankment where the ground is flat. I should see more from up there. I have to climb on all fours. My fingers are filthy. Water fights its way through the grass to the road at the bottom. A steady stream. It takes me more than a minute, but I reach the top and look down at the road. There are no emergency services, but they must be on their way. There's a bottleneck of traffic on the road heading out. People slowing down to get a better look. My leg seizes up with cramp. Pain shoots from my ankle to my calf to the tendons at the back of my knee. It makes me stop walking and shout out loud. Up ahead, the road is starting to clear and I've still not seen a thing. Just the lights and the rain. I turn and look back towards the garage. I can't see it anymore, but looking for it reminds me. Angelica's newspaper. It's in my inside pocket, sodden and sticking to the fabric. She won't want it like this. I stretch my leg until the cramp wears off. I stare at the heavy beams in the sky.

★ ★ ★

I turn the corner into Cressington Vale. It's still raining. Water pours down the street and gushes into drains. I walk past lights behind windows, their brightness determined by the thickness of the curtains between them. I stand outside Angelica's house. It looks empty. I walk to the front door, take out the cigarettes and the newspaper and go to put them through the letterbox. But it won't open. It's been taped up with coloured gaffer tape. Black, green and yellow. She must have done it herself. I put the cigarettes back in my pocket and carry the newspaper across the road. I open my front gate and look at Kipling's grave. It's full of nuts. I need to put some grass seed down. I look up at the bedroom window. Georgina's room is in darkness, but there's a light on downstairs. I must have forgotten to switch it off. It's a waste of electricity. I try to turn the key in the door, but it has nowhere to go. The door is already unlocked. I twist the handle and step into the house. It feels cold. Someone's turned the heating down. I can hear the kettle boiling. It must be Judy. She's come back to find Georgina. I take off my jacket, hang it on the banister and walk slowly to the kitchen. The door is slightly ajar. I can smell cinnamon. And Angelica. She's sat at the table, dressed in black from head to toe. Jacket and trousers.

'You didn't come to the funeral,' she says. 'Where have you been?'

'I couldn't face it. There's been an accident. How did you get in?'

'Are you all right?' she says.

And I think about it. Am I all right?

Well, I've spent the afternoon walking up and down a dual carriageway. Last week, I lost my two best friends. My wife is upstairs incarcerated by her second stroke in eighteen months. And Angelica is in my kitchen. She's wearing sweet perfume and

188

she's been looking through my manual. I'm soaking wet.

So am I all right? I guess not.

'Would you like a cigarette?' I ask her. 'Or a game of Travel Scrabble?'

Oracle

Angelica has opened the Travel Magic set and is pretending to be a magician. The three cups are upside down on the table. One of them has the wonderball underneath. She moves them, mixes them up and looks at me at the same time. Every so often her hands stop and she asks me which cup I think the ball is under. 'Which one this time?' she says. And I get it wrong because I'm not paying attention. I'm thinking about Georgina. I'm feeling guilty.

'I can't believe this only cost 99p,' she says. 'It's a shame about the newspaper. Have you been collecting the coupons too?'

'Yes,' I say, because it means I don't have to tell her I bought the newspaper for her. And she might not think I'm a pervert.

'You know today's was the last in the set?'

'Was it?'

'Yes, I cut mine out and sent them all off this morning. I'll get my free jar of coffee in twenty-eight days. They have to verify the coupons.'

'Does that mean I'm too late?'

'You're in luck actually. I normally buy

190

three papers and I picked up the same one twice.'

'That's handy.'

'You can have the spare, if you like.'

'Thanks. Georgina drinks coffee,' I say. It isn't true. She's never liked coffee. Or tea.

'Great. I'll fetch it for you later.'

The kettle rumbles on the worktop and switches itself off. Angelica gets up off her chair and walks to the cupboard by the fridge. Her bag is propped against the radiator behind her, where Kipling used to lie. It's black like her suit. Georgina's manual is still on the table. Neither of us has mentioned it. But she must've had a look.

'Where are your mugs?' she says.

'Second shelf up from the bottom.'

'So they are. Shall I make us some tea?'

'Yes, please.'

I sit down at the kitchen table and watch Angelica making tea. Water drips from my hair and onto my cheeks. It feels like I'm sweating. I wipe my face with a tea towel.

'Milk and sugar?'

'Just milk.'

She puts my drink in front of me. Her fingernails are black. She probably painted them for the funeral. One of them is shorter than the rest. I take my suit jacket off and hang it on the back of my chair. The cigarette packet falls out the pocket. Angelica picks it up, puts it on the table and sits opposite.

'I didn't think you smoked,' she says. I don't know how to respond. I could tell her that I bought them for her, or I could lie. I don't know which is worse.

'I bought them for you.'

'Oh, okay. That's kind.'

'They're quite strong, apparently.'

Water drips down the back of my neck. I need to change my clothes. I need to check on Georgina. But I can't. I can't leave Angelica. She might follow me up the stairs. I wrap the tea towel around my shoulders and watch her take a box of matches from her bag. She pulls a cigarette from the packet with her mouth, tightens her lips around the end, strikes a match and lights it first time.

'So, where've you been?'

'For a walk.'

'We waited for you. Morris said a few words in your place.'

'Morris Webster?'

'Yes.'

'They hardly knew each other.'

'They used to talk over the garden fence.'

'How do you know?'

'Morris told us. You should've been there.'

The rain is beating at the window. It sounds like someone throwing gravel at the glass. I hold my hands tight around my mug. What if Georgina smells the smoke? It could be ghosting up the staircase, into her room and lungs. I lean forward in my chair, rest my arms on the table and use my heel to shut the kitchen door.

'You look freezing,' says Angelica.

'I'll get changed in a minute.'

I don't know what to say to her. I try not to look in her direction. She's looking at me and smoking. The manual is between us. And the wonderball. Three upturned cups. Georgina will be awake. She'll be worrying about me. I know she worries about me. I stare at the kitchen window, mud smeared across the glass, probably from a football. I need to clean it. I can hear Angelica breathing, sucking in air. A cloud of smoke drifts across my eye line. A thin mist of swirls.

'How's Georgina?' she says. The words cut through me. I feel my skin tighten. She's read the manual. She's seen the blender on the worktop. She's listened to my lies. The ambulance is on its way.

'How did you get in?'

'John used the key you gave him. We wanted to make sure you were okay.'

'That was years ago. Did you go upstairs?'

'John shouted but got no answer. His

dinner was ready. He had to go. I said I'd wait on my own. I haven't been here long. I hope you don't mind.'

'How do you know about Georgina?'

'Don told me. A couple of weeks ago.'

'What did he say?'

'Nothing.'

'He must've said something.'

'I understand if you don't want to talk about it.'

'What did he tell you?'

'That she had a stroke. He just said she'd had a stroke.'

Angelica looks away from me. She never looks away from me. She always keeps eye contact. I've got this written down. Sometimes she closes her eyes when she laughs and I can see the make-up on her eyelids. But she never looks away. She never seems uncomfortable. Not like this.

'What else did he say?'

'He just said she'd had a stroke last year. And that she'd just about recovered. I was only asking. I didn't mean to upset you.'

'She's at my mum and dad's.'

'Okay.'

'That's why you've not seen her.'

'Okay, that makes sense. People have been worried.'

'She's fine.'

194

'Of course. Where do your mum and dad live?'

'Halfton Bridge.'

'Where's that?'

'About ten miles from here. It's on the other side of the motorway.'

'Is that where you grew up?'

'No, they moved when Georgina's mother died.'

'That must've been quite recently.'

'It was twenty years ago.'

'Really? How old was she?'

'Fifty-six.'

'Shit. That's young. What happened?'

'She had a stroke.'

'Oh,' she says, and looks away again, 'I see.'

We sit in silence for a few seconds. It feels like forever. Then Angelica puts her hand on the manual, arches her neck and breathes smoke into the air, up and behind her, away from me on purpose. She turns the manual ninety degrees. I can see the red cross on the spine. I coloured it in with a felt tip pen. A blue 'G' in the centre. G is for Georgina. My sweet Georgie.

'This is amazing,' she says. 'It's so detailed. It must've been incredibly difficult for you. There's so much to remember.'

'That's why I wrote it down.'

'I guess so. I'm glad she's feeling better.'

I don't reply. My eyes are watering. It's the smoke. Angelica is staring at me. She looks concerned. She thinks that I'm upset. I shouldn't have bought the cigarettes. I rub my face with the towel and take a sip from my tea. Let's talk about something else. What can we talk about? I could tell her the truth. Ask her to help me. But I'm not ready. Not yet. The argument. Angelica's argument with Benny. That's what we should talk about. I'd completely forgotten.

'I heard about the fight,' I say.

'What fight?'

'You and Benny Martin. In the street.'

'I don't know what you're talking about.'

'Don said he saw you. Before he died.'

'Well he was wrong. There was no fight.'

'Are you sure? He seemed pretty certain.' Angelica put her palms on the table, leaned towards me and looked me straight in the eye. I wanted to look away. But I couldn't. She wouldn't let me.

'Gordon. Listen to me. There was no fight. Don was wrong. Now let's just leave it. Okay? Let's move on.' She paused a moment, held her glare. I didn't respond to her question. She didn't want a response. We were moving on.

Note: No information provided. Engineer conversation with Benny. Before school. Approach with caution. Risk factor = 8. Note end.

Angelica has gone. She left an hour ago with a slice of buttery cinnamon cake. But she'll be back. She needs to give me a newspaper I don't really want, and coupons I don't really collect. She needs to return the plate she took the cake on. I've spoken to Georgina. She doesn't suspect a thing. She's taken her tablets and eaten her dinner. I've done her exercises. We've played noughts and crosses. She squeezed my hand to ask me why my hair was wet. I told her it was raining outside. I said, 'Can't you hear it?' and she just lay there. I sat with her until her eyes closed. Then I stood by the curtain, waited for her breathing to deepen, kept an eye out for Angelica. She'd said she wouldn't be back for a while. 'I could do with a bath first,' she said. 'Do you mind waiting for an hour or two?' And I'd said, 'Perfect, there's no rush,' and watched her walk across the road in the rain, her jacket round the cake like a cape.

I left Georgina, pulling her door tightly shut. I walked to the spare room, took my files from the bookshelf and put them into piles on the bed. I used the handle on her old umbrella to pull the ladder down from the loft. I climbed up and into darkness, ran my hand along the wall and found the light switch, made my fingers black with dust. I stepped carefully to the back of the room, ducked under beams, moved Georgina's mother's Christmas decorations, found some empty boxes. They were flat, single pieces of cardboard. I had to fold them into shape and tape them up at the bottom. I lined them up on the landing, filled them with files and wrote on the sides with marker pen. I labelled them from A to Z. Then I picked them up again, one by one, and put them back in the loft. It took me another hour.

On my way back down I found a box of jewellery and a file I didn't recognise. They were under the tent with the hole in the roof. The box contained necklaces, my mother's old watch and Georgina's wedding ring, which she had to stop wearing when her fingers swelled up. The file had 'Homework' written on the spine. It was in Georgina's handwriting. The sheets inside weren't attached to the folder. They were held together with an elastic band and had dates in the margins. They were written three years ago. I licked my thumb and flicked through the pages. She'd been learning another language. English in blue pen. Russian in red. Numbers, colours and greetings. And she'd never thought to tell me. It must have been a surprise.

Pretending

It's now fifteen minutes past eleven. Angelica is yet to arrive. I'm standing by the window looking out at the street and into her living room. She hasn't closed her curtains properly. I can see the back of an armchair and a section of fireplace. There are pictures in frames on the mantelshelf, but I can't tell who or what they are. The light in the room keeps changing. It flickers, makes shapes on the wall. She must be watching television. I stand up, put my hands on my hips and stretch my back. It hurts from all the lifting and the walking in the rain. It's over six hours since Angelica left. It's getting late. I'm beginning to think she's not coming. I should feel relieved, but I don't. I want her to come back. I want us to play Travel Scrabble. I want to get to know her better. Just in case I need her.

* * *

It's five past midnight. The rain has stopped. Cressington Vale is covered in puddles and John Bonsall's lawn has flooded. Petals float across the surface of the water and out into the street. Angelica is sitting on her doorstep. She has a glass of milk in her hand. She's still wearing her funeral clothes, which means she lied when she said she wanted a bath. I can see her fingernails when she puts the glass to her mouth. Black ovals on pale white skin. She said she'd come back. How could she forget? I think about knocking on the window and waving. Then she'll have to come over. It would be rude not to. I make a fist with my hand, step slowly from behind the curtain, stop and go back to where I was. I can't let her see me. No-one can see me. I look at the sky. Dark and starless. Hidden by layers of cloud. Then at Angelica once more. She stands up and runs her palms down the sides of her suit trousers. She turns around and goes into the house, leaves the door wide open. I watch her walk away down the hall. She disappears for more than a minute and returns wearing her long, black, fluffy-cuffed coat and her hair tied back. She has a newspaper under her arm. I knew she wouldn't forget.

★ ★ ★

'Would you like a cup of tea?' I ask. Angelica's in my kitchen again. She's leaning against the wall and warming her hands on the radiator. 'Yes please,' she says. I fill the kettle with water.

'I thought you weren't going to bother.'

'Yes, sorry it's late. I could see your light on, so I guessed you were still up.'

'Which light?'

'I don't know. Probably the landing. My toilet won't flush.'

'What have you done to it?'

'Nothing. I've been at it all night. It worked fine this morning.'

'It's the rain.'

'What do you mean?'

'The rain's messed with your plumbing.'

'How?'

'I've no idea, but whenever it rains like it did today, something usually happens to someone.'

'Really?'

'Ina Macaukey's drains burst last year. It stank to high heaven.'

'I think I'll ring someone in the morning.'

'And the water's always brown.'

'I can't say I've noticed.'

We're standing on opposite sides of the room. I don't feel guilty anymore. Georgina's upstairs and she's fine. No better, no worse. Instead, I feel anxious. It's Angelica's fault. She's not like she was before. She seems anxious too. Her eyes are fixed on the table between us, the newspaper open at the page with the coupon. She scrapes one of her high heels back and forth along the floor tiles, slowly and without a sound. The kettle spits and gurgles as the water starts to boil. I should never have mentioned Benny before. She's still annoyed at me.

'Tea's ready,' Angelica puts her elbows to the wall and pushes herself upright. She pulls a chair out and sits down at the table. I take two mugs from the draining board. The mugs we drank from this afternoon.

'Gordon,' she says. 'Does Georgina know about Don?'

'Know what?'

'Have you told her he's passed away?'

'No, not yet.'

'He spoke of her kindly, you know.'

'She's still upset about Kipling. It would be too much.'

'Would she not have liked to have been at the funeral?'

'She hates funerals.'

'Okay, it's just that Morris said . . . '

'Morris knows nothing. She wouldn't have been well enough.'

'I thought she was fighting fit again.'

'She is. She's fine. She's been well looked after.'

This is not what I expected. I'm being rude. Why is she asking me questions about Georgina? She's never met her. We should talk about something else. But now I'm thinking about Don, dead in his shed. Kipling in the sink. Georgina in her bed clothes.

'How long's she staying with your mum and dad? I'd love to meet her. She sounds like an incredible woman.'

'She is,' I say, without thinking about my answer first. I don't know where to look, so I try everywhere. At the walls, floor and ceiling. Through the kitchen window. At the clock on the front of the cooker. It reads 12:38 in the morning. The numbers made from short luminous lines.

'When's she coming back?'

'Soon,' I say. 'She'll be back soon.'

'Don said you sold your car.'

'I did.'

'I can drive you when you pick her up, if you like.'

'No, it's fine.'

'I don't mind.'

'Really, it's quite all right.'

'Well, I'm happy to help. Or I'm sure John would take you, if you'd prefer. I can ask him. It's no problem.'

'No, not John. I don't want John to take me.'

'I'll take you then. You've seen the car.'

This is too much. I want to tell her the truth. I want to say, she's not at my mum and dad's because I haven't spoken to them for more than a year. They don't know the half of it and that's the way they like it. Georgina's upstairs. She's had another stroke and I'm looking after her. That's right, another stroke. Do you want to help me? Do you? Fine. Thought not. Let's eat cake and do magic.

'That's very kind of you,' I say. 'I'll let you know when she's ready.' Angelica smiles without opening her mouth, nods her head and folds her arms. She leans back on her chair and balances it on two legs. The toes of her shoes on the floor. She looks like a child in a classroom. Causing trouble. Being naughty.

'Okay,' she says. 'Sounds like a plan.'

I drink my tea in three long gulps. It burns my tongue and throat. I'll probably get an ulcer.

'Would you like another cup of tea?'

'I've not started this one yet. You must be thirsty.'

'How about some more magic?'

'No, I need my beauty sleep. I just wanted to bring the paper over. I'll be off once I've drunk my drink.'

'But you've only just got here.'

'It's very late.'

'That doesn't matter.'

'Remember to send your coupons off tomorrow. There's a closing date.' She reaches for her drink and loses her balance. She falls forward in her chair. Its front legs crash to the floor. She waits a moment, checks she's still in one piece. Then she laughs out loud. She has metal-coloured fillings in her back teeth. Each and every one of them, left side and right. I can't believe I've not noticed before.

Note: When brushing, always stand to the side or behind. Keep one hand free to support the jaw. Adopt a gentle, repetitive motion. Excess toothpaste can be spat without rinsing. Bowl necessary. Note end.

Angelica finishes her tea. She stands up and shakes her ponytail. This hasn't gone to plan. Too much sitting in silence. Too much talk of Georgina. The clock on the cooker says 12:51. I don't know why she's stayed so long. I'm not sure why she came at all. I bet John Bonsall put her up to it. I bet they feel sorry for me, because I missed the funeral. They think I'm upset. They want to fetch Georgina from my Mum and Dad's. They want to make sure we're all right. The both of us. Me and my wife. Always asking questions. Always being helpful. I bet Judy's in on it too. Being kind. Poking her nose in.

'Would you like some more cake on a plate?'

'No, thank you. I've not eaten the first piece yet. Plus I'll get fat.'

'You're not fat.'

'No, I said I'll get fat.'

'Not for your age.' She stops and glares. I try to smile. 'You know what I mean,' I say. 'Not like that.' And her mouth softens. She wraps her coat tight around her waist. She nods and smiles.

'Can I use your toilet?'

'Yes.'

'Are you sure?'

'Yes, it's fine. Honestly.'

'I don't want to risk mine.'

'It's no problem.'

Of course it's a problem. Georgina's door could have opened when the draught came in with Angelica. She could be awake and waiting for me to sit with her. For me to make sure she's taken her medication. For me to keep her alive. Angelica walks across the kitchen. I need to go with her. I need to check Georgina's door.

'Which one is it?' she says. I follow her, put my arm across her chest and stop her from climbing the stairs.

'Would you mind if I go first? I'm desperate.'

'Really?'

'Yes.'

'Okay. Shall I wait on the landing?' I put my hand on the rail, climb halfway up the stairs and look through the gaps in the banister. Georgina's door is closed. I feel my heart rate slow a little.

'Yes, that's fine. I'll be quick.'

Angelica follows me upstairs. I open the bathroom door and step inside, lock it behind me. I empty the glass that I keep my tooth-brush in and rinse it under the tap. Then I hold the glass against the door, press my ear to the bottom and listen to Angelica's foot-steps. She's pacing the landing. She's humming to herself. I hope she doesn't sing. It'll be too loud. It'll wake Georgina. When can I open the door? How long does it take to go to the toilet? I've never timed it. Another ten sec-onds maybe. That should do the job. The footsteps stop. So does the humming. I put the glass back on the corner of the bath in the exact same position. A dark ring to guide me. I put my toothbrush in it, walk back across the bathroom and unlock the door. I open it as slowly and as quietly as possible. Angelica's in the spare room. She's standing next to the curtain looking out across the street. She's standing where I stand.

'Your turn,' I whisper, but she ignores me. I walk across the landing, wrap my fingers round the door frame, turn the light on with my thumb. Our reflections appear in the window. She glares via the glass.

'Turn it off.' Her arms are folded and her hands are clasped around her shoulder blades. I can see her wedding ring.

'I said, turn it off.' And this time I do. I sit on the end of the bed with my head in my hands. Angelica sits down next to me.

'That's Benny,' she says.

'I know.'

'What's he doing?'

'He's painting.'

'With his eyes closed.'

'Yes.'

She stands up again, turns 360 degrees around the room. She looks up and down the walls. At the single bed and its slept-in sheets. At the empty bookcase. I should have gone to the funeral. I can hear Don's pockets rattling, somewhere in the distance. His whistling in the street. Angelica looks at me through the darkness. I can see the whites of her eyes changing shape, getting thinner as they close. I think she's smiling. She puts her hand on the curtain.

'What else can you see?' she says.

Practice

My father was a ballroom dancer. He took it up when he got made redundant. He said losing his job was the best thing that could have happened to him. These were going to be the best years of his life. It was time to do something different. He'd been sat in that lorry for far too long. He told us his plans over Christmas dinner, a forkful of stuffing in one hand, a glass of whiskey in the other. We all laughed at him. Georgina made jokes about his weight. My mother called him a stupid old man. I slapped him on the back and told him he'd never live it down. We took it in turns to make fun at his expense. All of us except Mary, who said nothing. She smiled politely and sometimes laughed along. But she never joined in. She simply sat in her chair and drank gin by the glassful, her party hat skewed on her head.

Three weeks into January, she became my father's dance partner. They had lessons at the leisure centre. It was fifteen miles away, but that didn't matter. My father loved it. He got himself a suit fitted and bought a pair of expensive shoes. He polished them every day.

I asked him if anyone else wore a suit just for lessons. He said, 'No, only me.' They went every Monday for the first six months, then Thursdays as well after that. He talked of mambos and boleros, quicksteps and competitions. She barely mentioned it at all. Georgina said it was because her mother was shy. She didn't like to show off like my father did. 'That's funny,' I said. 'It never used to bother her.'

★   ★   ★

When my mother turned sixty, my father threw a party. They had it at home, the house I grew up in. Georgina baked a birthday cake. I helped her squeeze the icing and watched her place cherries around the edge. Artificial flowers in the centre. The house was full of people, everyone tightly packed into the living room. My mother cleared the furniture especially, pushing the sofa to the wall to leave a space in the middle. She packed away her ornaments. My father turned the television round. He'd invited most of his old workmates. I didn't recognise any of them. Nobody knew who they were. They all looked the same. Large and full of ale. There were five women there. Georgina, her mother, my mother and two of my mother's friends. One was called Jackie, the other Barbara. They sat in the corner, chatted away while my father proposed a toast.

'To my darling wife, happy birthday and God bless.' He raised his glass in the air. Everyone else did the same. My mother blushed. The man next to me, one of my father's workmates, leaned over to me and whispered, 'Which one's his piece then?' and I looked up at him, shook my head and said, 'I don't know. I'm his son.' He stood and stared at me. Then he laughed, said, 'Of course you are. I'm just joking with you.' I nodded and mustered a smile. We stood next to each other and said nothing more until my father finished his speech. Then he turned to me again, looked uncomfortable, said, 'Cheers pal,' and left to get another can of beer from the kitchen.

At midnight, we made my father dance with Georgina's mother. At first they'd both refused. They said they were too drunk. Not enough practice. Everyone would laugh. But we wouldn't let it go. My father's workmates were remorseless. They teased him and swore in unison. 'Daft old bastard,' they called him. 'Ballroom dancing bollocks. Show us your fucking shoes.' My father laughed it off. He was used to it. But my mother wasn't. She got upset. She grabbed his arm and said, 'Why

212

not give it a go. It'll shut them up. Plus I've never seen you dance together.' Mary still said nothing. She just glared at my father. It was his decision. This was his fault. 'All right, all right,' he said. 'Give me five minutes.'

My father left the room and went upstairs to get changed. He came back ten minutes later wearing his suit and shoes. He looked immaculate. He stood in the middle of the room and pointed at the record player. I lifted the needle and everyone cheered as the music started. My father held out his hand. Mary stood up and walked over to him. She let him hold her in his arms. And then they danced, moved around the room in fits and starts. We watched in disbelief, clutched our drinks and winced. They were terrible. Hopeless. When it was over, we applauded politely. No jokes. No swearing. It was that bad. Like they'd never had a lesson in their lives.

★ ★ ★

My father found Mary dead in the garden. She was lying on her front and wearing her dressing gown. It had ridden up above her knees as she'd fallen. Her legs were on show. They were yellow and blue. The ambulance came quickly, but it was far too late. She'd been there at least forty-eight hours, they said. Georgina blamed herself. She said she should have seen it coming. Her own mother, for God's sake.

'You're being silly,' I told her. 'It's just one of those things.'

'No, it's not, Gordon. It was only a matter of time. We knew everything. We could have done something. So could your father.'

'There's no use blaming him. It's no-one's fault.'

'You're wrong. We should have done something.'

My father stood with Georgina as they lowered Mary's coffin into the ground. He was devastated. It crippled him. He's never been the same. Three months after the funeral, he put the house up for sale. A month later they'd moved. Time for a change, he said. Too many memories. He was right, there were plenty of memories, but they weren't all bad. I grew up in that house. He wasn't the only person to live there. We lived there too. Me and my mother. Birthdays and Christmases. Easter eggs and Pancake Days. It was the place we returned to when we'd been on holiday. I remember at night, before I went to bed, the way my mother used to sit on the carpet, watching television. She said it was because of her eyes. They needed looking at. I remember my father sitting in his chair behind her, stroking her shoulders, sighing to himself and playing with her hair. And Sunday lunchtimes after church. My mother's roast dinners and Georgina's parents. All six of us sat round a table made for four.

The drinking. The laughter. The rumours.

I remember everything.

Quarantine

After her first stroke, when she'd learnt to talk again, Georgina said she wanted to dance. She thought it would improve her balance. It would do her some good. Doctor Richmoor told her she should take things one step at a time, but that she had to have something to aim for. She needed long-term goals and there was no reason why dancing couldn't be one of them. He retired last year, moved to New Zealand with his son and his family. Jonathan replaced him. There's more than forty years between them. He knew my mother and father, treated them for decades. And Georgina's parents too. He knew about her father's lungs, but stayed true to his word when asked not to tell. There was nothing he could do, he said, but wait.

It was Doctor Richmoor who helped Georgina. When she first came home from hospital, he organised everything. We trusted him implicitly. He made sure we had everything we needed, from specialists and social workers to bath rails and wheelchairs. Whenever someone new came to see us, he pencilled in a home visit. The speech therapist, nurse or whoever else was with Georgina would do what they had to do while he sat in the kitchen drinking soup from a mug. He never drank tea or coffee. Just like Georgina. And he never interfered unless I asked him to. When I did ask, he always reassured me, telling me they knew what they were doing. 'Watch and learn,' he used to say. When I told him I wanted to take early retirement, he went through my pension scheme and made sure that we got benefits. When I rang him in the middle of the night and told him Georgina had fallen out of bed, he got in his car and drove round in his pyjamas. When I told him I couldn't cope anymore, that I thought it might be best if Georgina moved to a nursing home, he spoke to me for more than an hour. He made his other patients wait, asked me to think about the progress she'd made, told me to start making lists. 'Write things down,' he said. 'It'll make life easier.'

Before he left for New Zealand, Doctor Richmoor came to visit. Georgina boiled the kettle and poured him a cup of soup. She did it all on her own. No bother at all. 'I'd love to learn to dance again,' she said. I smiled at her and thought about our parents. Doctor Richmoor smiled too. 'There's no reason why you can't,' he said. 'Just make sure you send me the photos.' We talked about the future. He was looking forward to the weather and spending time with his grandchildren. He said he didn't know if he'd ever return. I said I might go back to work, even though I didn't want to. And Georgina, after eighteen months of pain and rehabilitation, she just wanted to dance. To do something new. Something different. She was walking and talking, almost back to how she used to be. She made jokes about my files. She said they took up too much room. She was going to have a bonfire while I was out. We laughed about it. I said the files kept me sane and she laughed even more. But she never read them. She couldn't make out the words.

★　★　★

Only six weeks after Doctor Richmoor left the country, Georgina had her second stroke. He has no idea. Jonathan neither. He just checks me over and writes me her prescriptions. He reads her records, but he's never spoken to her. He asks me how she's doing, but he never comes round to see for himself. Jonathan is not like Doctor Richmoor. But he is a doctor. So I believe his every word. Sometimes, when he's checking my blood pressure or I'm reading his notice board, I think about telling him my secret. I wonder what would happen if I asked him for his help. I think about shaking him, shouting 'Why? Why has this happened to my wife? Why has this happened to me?' But there's no point. The damage has been done. I know the answers. I've heard them all before. It's because something stopped the blood supply from getting to her brain. It's because the same thing happened to her mother. It's because of the HRT. The menopause. The depression. Our failure to have children. It's what the Lord has chosen. There's nothing I could have done to stop it. Nothing I could have said to make a difference. I'm just here to pick up the pieces. And keep faith.

Doctor Richmoor sent two postcards. One was addressed to me, the other to Georgina. Mine had a map of New Zealand on it. Cities and towns marked out with pictures next to them. They'd arrived safely. The weather was terrific. They were all doing fine. Even the dogs. Georgina's postcard had a rugby player on the front. His hands in the air and a grimace on his face. He looked gigantic. 'New Zealand Tourism Board', it said in the top right hand corner. On the back, in gold marker pen, it said, 'Dear Georgina. Is this what

you had in mind?' She's not read it yet.
She's not smiled and shaken her head.
She's not had chance to reply.

It arrived a week too late.

I've filed it away for when she gets better.

Revelations

Angelica has confided in me. We are definitely friends.

It happened yesterday morning. She knocked on the front door while I was in the bedroom. I'd just finished bathing Georgina. 'There's someone at the door,' I told her. 'I'll be back in a minute.' I walked downstairs with my flannel. My hands were wet and soapy. As I reached the bottom I saw Angelica's fingers. They were inside the house, poking through the letterbox. She was holding it open from the outside and crouching to look through the hole. I could see the bridge of her nose and one of her eyes behind her hair.

'Hello,' she said. 'I didn't think you were home.'

I opened the door and Angelica barged past me. There was nothing I could do to stop her. She took off her coat and hung it over the banister. I followed her to the kitchen and tossed the flannel into the sink. I turned on the tap and washed the soap from my hands.

'What have you been up to?' she said.

'Cleaning,' I replied.

She plugged the kettle in at the wall, took a mug from the cupboard and a slice of cake from the fridge without asking. Chocolate sponge cake. Georgina's favourite. I'd made it for her as a treat and a test. But she didn't want to eat it. I thought she might have been ready. But apparently not. Angelica ate with her hand beneath her chin like a plate.

'You've got chocolate on your face.'

'Where?'

'Your cheek.'

'Has it gone?'

'The other cheek.'

'How about now?'

'No, you've made it worse.'

'You do it then.'

I dried my hands and walked over. She lifted her chin, half-closed her eyes and looked down her nose at me. I licked my thumb and wiped the chocolate away. She dragged her sleeve across her mouth when I'd finished.

'That's disgusting,' she said, and walked over to the window. 'Why is there a football in your garden?'

'It's from next door.'

'Which side?'

'Annie Carnaffan.'

'The old woman? Has she got grandchildren?'

'No. She hasn't.'

'What does the writing say?'

'What writing?'

'There's something written on the side of the ball.'

Angelica turned and tipped her head towards the window. I peered over her shoulder at the black markings on the football. She wanted me to go outside and get it. Annie Carnaffan had never written anything on any of the other footballs. Though I wouldn't have put it past her. Wicked old woman. I unlocked the back door, stepped outside and walked across the lawn. The grass was wet with dew and soaked my slippers. I picked the football up with my fingertips and carried it back inside to Angelica. She was finishing her cake.

'Well?' she said. 'What does it say?'

'It doesn't say anything.'

'Are you sure? It looked like it was done with a marker pen.'

'It's a picture. Of an eye. With lashes. I think she's finally lost it.'

Angelica scrunched her eyebrows and smirked, which I took to mean that she agreed with me, and that she wasn't going to ask any questions. I put the football on the table and walked back to my position by the door to the hall. Angelica stood opposite. I looked her up and down without her noticing. She was wearing her fluffy-cuffed coat and a scarf with multicoloured stripes that stretched from one end to the other. Too many colours to count. It covered her neck and jaw right up to her mouth. It was covered in crumbs.

'Anyway, I'm sorry to surprise you like this,' she said.

'It's all right,' I replied.

'I was thinking about the other day and thought I'd come over.'

'Which day do you mean?'

'After Don's funeral, when I was here. When I brought you the coupons?'

I paused before I answered. She knew something. She was on to me. First she'd seen Benny painting and then she'd found Georgina. Through a gap in the door. By the way I was standing. Somehow she knew. And now she was here to confront me. While eating my cake and wearing her scarf. I'd have to tell her everything.

'Okay,' I said. 'I remember.'

Angelica folded her arms and took two steps towards me. She was close enough to touch but far enough away for me to still have time to react. I reached down slowly, put my arm across the door and my fingers on the handle. I pretended to lean.

Angelica lowered her voice.

'Does he always paint with his eyes closed?' she said. I paused again, thought about my reply, made sure it wasn't a trick.

'Every night. Between one and two in the morning.' She smiled at me and I smiled back. I didn't know why we were smiling, but I knew that something was different. Her eyes had changed. They were kinder, like I could tell her anything.

'How often do you watch him?'

'Quite often, but not too much.'

'Do you think he knows that you watch him?'

'No. Nobody does. Only you.'

She closed her eyes and let her smile turn into a laugh. She unfolded her arms, pulled her scarf away from her chin.

'I'd like to watch Benny with you,' she said.

'Pardon?'

'Can I watch Benny with you? Would you mind?'

'Why? What for?'

'Just for a while. To see how he does it. To see what it's like.'

'I don't think so. It's nothing special.'

'It looked pretty special.'

'Not really. It helps me to sleep.'

'I know it's a lot to ask, but I won't stay long. I promise.'

'I don't think so. Sorry.'

Angelica took another step towards me. I tightened my grip on the handle and looked over her shoulder. It was starting to rain. Georgina's sheets needed washing. I'd have to dry them inside and make the house smell nice like the powder. Angelica moved her head to the side and into my line of vision. She tried to force my attention.

'If you let me watch him,' she said. 'I'll tell you why we were fighting.' We held each other's gaze and I let her lean towards me. She wanted to watch Benny with me. She wanted to tell me a secret. I let go of the door handle carefully, uncurled my fingers one at a time. This was what I'd hoped would happen. A chance to get to know each other properly. A chance for me to test out her credentials. She put one hand on my shoulder and shielded her mouth with the other. 'He kissed me,' she whispered, softly in my ear.

Restoration

I turn on the tap and fill the kitchen sink with warm water. Outside, the sunlight floods more than half of the garden, but there is still a section of lawn that's yet to see the day, where the frost waits for the warmth. I bend down, open the cupboard under the sink and take out the detergent that I bought yesterday. The bottle is bright pink and so is the liquid inside. It looks edible, like melted marshmallows or badly-made icing on a cake. I unscrew the cap, flip it over and fill it with detergent. I pour the detergent into the water and stir the mixture with my fingers. It's almost ten o'clock in the morning. Twenty minutes ago, I took my electric toothbrush from the bathroom. It has a blue plastic trim around the button. It's fully charged. I walked from the bathroom to the landing, climbed into the loft and collected Georgina's jewellery box. Her wedding ring needs cleaning.

Tonight is the night. Angelica is coming over and we are watching Benny together. I have taken precautions. Yesterday I came up with a plan to make sure that she doesn't find

Georgina. I went to B&Q, bought a new lock and screwed it to the bedroom door. I did it while Georgina was sleeping. She never even noticed and it won't change a thing. If Angelica asks, I'll tell her that the lock has been there for months and that I put it there for Kipling. That I kept him from the bedroom so he couldn't make a mess on the carpet. I will tell her that I still use the lock because I can't get out of the habit. It's a sensitive subject. We shouldn't talk about it. The plan is fool proof. I can still make notes — I'll just keep my files in the loft. I can still look after Georgina — I'll just need to keep up our secret. It all seems very straightforward.

I open the box of jewellery and take out Georgina's wedding ring. It is plain and silver, a simple band, the same as mine. It has tiny marks on the outside and a thin layer of grime in the middle. All of which will wash away. I close the lid and hold the ring up to the window. It glistens in the sunlight, despite the dirt and fingerprints. I place the ring in the sink and pick up the electric toothbrush. I use my thumb to switch it on. It spins and buzzes like a scaled-down chainsaw. I lower the toothbrush into the sink and watch it twirl and spin and flick water up and onto my trousers. There is no time to stop. Today is a busy day. I let the brush touch the ring, turning slowly, carefully, enough to scrub without scraping. After thirty seconds I take the ring out of the water and hold it to the light again. The marks and grease have all but disappeared. I repeat until satisfied.

Note: Dry ring with hairdryer. Wrap in cotton wool. Keep safe. Note end.

It was New Year's Eve. She was twenty-one and I was twenty-one in two days' time. We'd been with friends and were walking home through the centre of the village. Georgina was staying at my parents' house. She'd have my bed and I'd sleep downstairs on the sofa. I looked at my watch and told her we should go to the void. We should walk up to where we used to sit together, when we watched the machines. She said she didn't want to. It was cold. My parents would be waiting. I told her that they'd be in bed, that she could have my scarf and that I had a key to the house. We could let ourselves in when we wanted.

'Let's sit here,' I said. 'Just for a while.' She humoured me, but I didn't mind. There was something I needed to say. I wanted it to be special. Or as special as it could possibly be, all things considered. I talked and Georgina listened. She replied occasionally, but only so

I knew that she was paying attention. I sat behind her with my arms around her stomach and my chin resting on her shoulder. I could smell her perfume. The evening's cigarette smoke in her hair. I pointed towards the hill on the opposite side of the void. Back then it had been a heap of soil, now it was covered in grass. 'Can you remember the first time we came here?' I said. 'We sat over there.' Georgina leaned forward, turned her head and looked at me. 'Of course,' she said, and stood up without using her hands. 'We should get going.' I stayed where I was. I didn't want to leave. 'Come on,' she said. 'It's freezing.' She bent down, put her arm under mine and tried to drag me to my feet, but I resisted. I watched her tighten the knot on my scarf around her neck. She turned and walked away.

'Wait,' I said. Georgina turned again. 'I wanted to ask you something.' She put her hands on her hips and waited for me to continue. Her hair was longer then. She wore it down over her shoulders. I stared at her and tried to speak. But the words had dried. I sat with my mouth wide open, unable to say what I wanted to say. Georgina filled the gap. She'd read me like a book.

'You want to marry me?

'Yes. Yes please.' She looked away from me.

Just for a second. And then back. She smiled with her eyes. That's how I remember it.

'Gordon, I'm not pregnant anymore,' she said. 'They'll never know unless we tell them. It wasn't meant to be. Nothing needs to change.'

I paused. Kept eye contact. Made sure she knew I was serious.

* * *

I'm standing at the window and I'm waiting for Angelica. It's ten minutes to one in the morning and she is in the process of leaving her house. One by one the lights are going out. First upstairs, now downstairs. My fingers are twitching and no matter how much I concentrate, I can't seem to get them to stop. I must be nervous. Another light goes out. And then a different light comes back on. It's upstairs, which means she must have forgotten something. Or she's decided to go to the toilet.

I know that having Angelica here is a risk, but I need to learn more about her. I need to know that she is capable of helping me care for Georgina, in case something happens. Something I haven't prepared for. I'm ready for Angelica's arrival, but I don't know if it's good enough. What if she talks or laughs too loudly? What if she shouts, swears or drops something? There is much that can go wrong. But I'm still looking forward to it. All the lights are out. The door is opening. Here she is. Jeans and t-shirt, arms folded, into the night.

'Are you sure you wouldn't like tea?'

'No thank you, Gordon. Still no thank you. You've already asked me twice.'

'Yes. Sorry.'

Angelica smiles, sniffs and looks at the kitchen clock. She's twitched and glanced and checked the time on seven occasions in the four minutes that's she's been here. It may be more because I had my back to her when I poured myself a drink. We've barely said a word because we don't know what to say to each other. Not like before, when we spoke freely and played Scrabble. She must be nervous too. It's probably down to Benny. And everything that happened.

'Gordon, it's almost one o'clock.'

'Really? Already?'

'Won't we miss the start?' I pull back my sleeve and tap the face of my watch. I look at the clock on the wall. It feels strange her being here. At this time. For Benny.

'Can I ask you a question?'

She sighs a little. She seems impatient. 'Go on,' she says. 'Okay.'

'When Benny kissed you.' I pause and wait

232

for her to acknowledge the subject matter. She nods silently. 'When Benny kissed you, did you kiss him back?' Angelica doesn't reply straight away. She allows the corners of her mouth to shape into the smallest of smiles. She holds my gaze and I begin to regret my question. It could have waited. It doesn't matter why she's here. Just that she is. Eventually she answers.

'Of course not, Gordon. He's just a boy.' She says it without losing the smile, which makes it difficult to tell if it's the truth or not. It seems intentional.

'Absolutely,' I say. 'And yes. We should get going.'

Angelica stands up, but I move quickly and get to the door before her. She follows me into the hall. I stop at the foot of the stairs and she almost walks into me. I turn and smile. She doesn't smile back. We climb the stairs and I walk slowly and carefully so that she must do the same. So that both of us tread quietly. I step onto the landing and into the spare room. We look through the window and across the street. At Benny's candles, dancing in the half-light. Angelica puts her hand on my shoulder and gently moves me aside. She stands by the curtain and watches.

One hour later she thanks me. She says she'll come back tomorrow.

Rhythms

It's half past one in the morning. Georgina is asleep and Angelica is sitting next to me on the bed in the spare room. Benny is painting. We're watching him together. We've watched him every day this week. I don't know what happened between them and I've decided I don't really care. I've started a new file and hidden it under the bed. It has everything in it. The times Angelica comes over and the clothes that she wears. The things she says and how long she stays for. I write them down as soon as she leaves. I watch her walk across the road and into her house. She waves when she closes her door.

Benny has stopped painting and is standing with his hands on his hips. Angelica hasn't spoken for over ten minutes. She's just been sitting there, staring out of the window. I arch my neck and look at the sky. It's perfectly clear. A full moon.

'What a beautiful night,' I say.

'Yes.'

'Look at the stars.'

'I know.'

'Aren't they bright?'

'I suppose.'

'You don't seem impressed.'

'I guess I've seen them before.'

Benny puts his paintbrush on the window-sill and walks to the dark side of his room. The side the light from the candles can't reach. We watch him fade away. Then he disappears completely. He must've gone to the toilet. He can't have finished painting.

'Is that it?' says Angelica.

'No, he'll come back. The candles are lit.'

'Where's he gone?'

'I don't know.'

She links her hands, holds the back of her head, yawns and stretches her shoulders. This is how it's been. We stand in silence for most of the time. Then she'll ask me about Benny. About his painting or how long we've got before he stops and packs his things away. Before she has to go again. I answer her politely and attempt to think of questions of my own. But I very rarely ask them. She makes me feel uncomfortable.

Note: Arrived = 12:54. Jeans (again), cream blouse. Conversations = 3. Departure = 02:04. Little progress. Note end.

'There he is. I told you he'd be back.'

'Is he limping?'

'Yes, he is.'

'How come?'

'He always limps.'

'I've never noticed.'

'It's not that bad.'

'What happened?'

'A dog attacked him.'

'Really?'

'Yes.'

'Not Kipling?'

'No, not Kipling. It was a dog from the estate. Beech Avenue.'

'What did it do?'

'He was walking home from school. It jumped at him and dug its teeth into his ankle.'

'Is that all?'

'It wouldn't let go.'

'What do you mean it wouldn't let go?'

'I mean it wouldn't let go. He had to go to hospital.'

'Bollocks. You're lying.'

'It's true. That's why he limps.'

'And does he really steal?'

'No. I made that up.'

Angelica shakes her head and half-laughs. It's the longest conversation we've had since we started watching Benny together. She doesn't know whether to believe me or not. I wish she wouldn't swear so much. She turns back to the window. The moonlight takes years off her. It reminds me where we are and what we're doing. We're sat on a bed together. We hardly know each other. And we're talking. We're finally talking.

'Have you ever had any pets?' I ask.

'Once.'

'What did you have?'

'A cat.'

'What was it called?'

'Patch.'

'That's nice.'

'It got hit by a car.'

I open my mouth to reply. Nothing comes out. I think about asking her what type of car it was. But I don't. I just stare out the window at Benny. He's stopped painting again. One of his candles is out. It's quarter to two in the morning and he'll soon be finishing up for the night. Angelica will be leaving.

'Are you sure his eyes are always closed?' she says.

'Absolutely.'

'Sometimes it's difficult to tell. It's pretty dark.'

'You get used to it.'

'I suppose so. Do you think he's had enough?'

'I don't know. Maybe.'

'Have you heard from Georgina? Is she

coming home soon?'

Unbelievable. We've spent an entire week together with barely a passing comment, and now she asks me that. Like she knows her. Like Georgina's an old friend that she's looking forward to seeing again. I don't know how to reply. If I say no she might well ask me again tomorrow. And then the next day. She'll start to get suspicious. I need a different answer. One that's not the truth.

'Next week,' I say. Another lie. I regret it instantly.

'How's she getting here?'

'I don't know.'

'We can pick her up in my car.'

'You don't need to do that.'

'It's fine.'

'I couldn't.'

'Don told me to keep an eye on you. I'm happy to help.'

Benny is taking his canvas down and putting his paintbrush and paints away. I've watched him do it more times than I care to remember. Angelica's hand is on my knee. She's being sympathetic. She's pretending to care about me. This is not what I expected. I don't know what I expected.

'Have you thought about telling his mother?' I ask.

'Telling whose mother what?'

'Benny's mother. About the kiss.'

'Why would I do that?'

'I suppose she might like to know what happened.'

Her eyes narrow in the dark. She's deciding how to answer and wondering why I'm changing the subject. She wants to do the same thing now herself. Benny has finished painting. It's time for her to go.

'So next week then,' she says, standing up. We watch Benny walk over to his bedroom window, put his palm on the glass and blow out his candles. 'It's a date.'

I should tell her to mind her own business or tell her the facts. But it's too soon for that. Instead I say nothing and follow her downstairs. She picks up her coat from the banister and wraps it around her shoulders. She ties her scarf around her neck. I switch on the hall light. It hurts my eyes. They need time to adjust. Angelica squints and it makes the lines on her forehead stand out. She looks forty-two again. I remove the chain and hold the door open. She squeezes past me and puts her hand on my chest for a moment. I force a smile. She smiles back and turns to walk away. Then she stops. She turns again.

'How did they remove the dog?' she says.

'Drugs,' I reply.

Spillage

Georgina doesn't know about Angelica. She is sleeping more than ever. When she is awake we go through our routines. If she's feeling up to it, I'll talk to her. Then she'll talk back as best she can, or use our system. I sat with her last night and ate my dinner. I handed Georgina a yoghurt, but she refused to take it. I peeled back the lid, scooped some out with a spoon and put it to her mouth. She slowly turned her head away. I asked her what the matter was. Did she want something else? Had I done something wrong? But she wouldn't speak to me. She didn't even try. Her face was pale. Her pulse was slow. She looked awful.

* * *

It's seven o'clock in the morning and I'm sitting on a cushion in the loft. The room is lit by an old-fashioned desk lamp that used to belong to Georgina's father. The lamp is metal painted beige with a dark brown button. It's attached to an extension lead that runs from the loft to the plug socket in the spare room. It's been up here for more than thirty years and I can't believe that it works. My files are still in boxes. I've cut the tape with scissors and lined them up against the wall in alphabetical order. Spines facing upwards. I woke up early to transcribe last night's events. Angelica was here again. She's been here every night this week. We're developing routines. She boils the kettle and I make the tea. Hers is the curtain on the right. Mine's the one on the left. It's all perfectly normal. There is nothing to worry about. Sometimes we talk. Sometimes we're silent. It depends on her mood and I don't mind either way. She's only here to watch Benny.

Last night Angelica wore an evening dress and earrings. Both were black and sparkled. Five hours earlier she'd left her house and walked to the end of Cressington Vale. She stood there for more than eighteen minutes. Checking her watch and adjusting her dress. I made notes while my malt loaf burned in the oven. I left it for as long as I could. When the smoke started creeping into the hall I put down my pen and rushed to the kitchen. I took the loaf from the oven and scraped it into the bin. It was black at the edges and completely ruined. When I went back to the window, Angelica had gone. She returned at five to one in the morning, came straight to our front door.

'Where have you been?' I asked. She took off her coat and sat next to me on the bed. Her dress was covered in glitter. Benny was lighting his candles.

'Out.'

'Where to?'

'Nowhere you'd know. He's almost ready to start.' She held her mug by the handle, walked to the curtain and waited for Benny. I began to repeat my question, but stopped before the words arrived. I asked her something else instead.

'Why do you go to the surgery so often?' She turned and looked at me. The room was dark and my eyes had yet to adjust. It was hard to gauge her reaction.

'You're nosy tonight.'

'I just wondered, that's all. I've never asked you.'

'Why would you ask me?'

'I don't know.'

'It's a very personal question, Gordon.'

'It wasn't meant to be.'

Angelica looked at the floor. It was a private matter. Women's troubles or something similar. I shouldn't have asked. I should have known better. It's none of my business. Not really. Not yet.

'Depression,' she said, without flinching. The silence seemed to last for minutes. 'And athlete's foot.' Her mouth cracked and formed a smile. 'What do you go for?' I tried to think of a joke of my own, but nothing felt amusing. Instead, I told her the truth.

'I don't anymore.'

Benny closed his eyes, outstretched his arm, placed his brush on the canvas and started painting. I stood up and joined Angelica at the window. She slurped her tea at approximately thirty-second intervals. It made it hard to concentrate. I almost asked her to stop. We were watching Benny together. He was painting pictures. She was keeping me company.

Note: Possible slurping solutions a) cool with extra milk b) use thinner mug c) suggest more patience required. Risk factor = 8. Note end.

I'm still in the loft. It's now seven fifteen and no longer dark outside. I can tell by the change in the light from the hole in the floor to the landing. I finish my notes, close Angelica's file and put it back in the appropriate box. The loft is cramped and the roof is covered in foam. It keeps the cold out and the heat in. If I want to walk to the other side of the room I have to tread carefully. The wooden beams are stable but the spaces in between won't hold my weight. One false step and I might fall through the floor and into the bedroom. My cushion is placed on a plank of wood that bridges one of the gaps. It makes my back ache. More than the chair in the bedroom.

I reach for the file that contains Georgina's homework. I've decided to teach myself Russian. When she gets better, we can do it together. First she'll learn to talk again. Then she'll finish what she started. It might take years. But that's what we'll do. This is my first lesson. The pages at the front of the file don't make any sense, so I flick through and search for some instructions. The final page is a glossary of terms with Russian words next to English translations. It has a photograph stuck to the front, Sellotape over the corners. In it are Georgina, Georgina's mother, my parents and me. We're pulling faces and pointing at the camera. There is Russian in the margin. Arrows leading to each of us. I don't know what they mean. We look like a family.

I unpeel the tape and hold the photograph up to the light. I remember when it was taken. My father was working again. He'd found a job at the local shop. It was ten minutes walk from their new house. We'd gone in and asked his boss to take a picture. We wanted to cheer him up and make him smile. He'd said he didn't want to work there. He'd said it was degrading and his friends would laugh. But he had no choice. My parents needed the money. He'd been one of only three drivers to lose their jobs when they began to run out of coal at Gutterton Half. They told him it was one of those things. He'd done little wrong. There was nothing they could do. So he took the job at the shop and worked there until he retired. Twenty years later. The morning after Georgina had her first stroke. He rang me to celebrate.

'It's my last day tomorrow, Gordon.'

'Yes Dad, I know.'

'No more early mornings for me.'

'Good for you.'

'I've got all the time in the world.'

'Dad I can't talk to you at the moment.' He started to say something else, but stopped. We didn't speak for several seconds. I'd upset him. He didn't like my tone. But I didn't care. 'I'm sorry, I have to go.' I waited for him to reply. Still nothing. He wanted an apology. I didn't offer. Eventually he spoke.

'Keep faith, Son,' he said. 'Keep faith.'

★ ★ ★

I've spent thirty minutes learning Russian. Georgina must have put her latest work at the front of the file, which means the basic material is all at the back. So far, I've mastered numbers one to ten and several colours. I copied them out and started a file of my own. R is for Russian. I stand up slowly to make sure I don't bang my head on the roof. I press the button on the lamp with my foot. It flickers half-light into the room then fizzles into darkness. I climb down from the loft and onto the landing.

Georgina is asleep in the bedroom. In fifteen minutes I will need to wake her up, help her drink her water, help her take her tablets, ask if she wants breakfast. Sunlight floods through the spare room window and illuminates the dust in the air. Particles swirl and fall. They are usually invisible. I walk into the light and check the street for activity. Nothing is happening. Cressington Vale is perfectly calm. I go back to the landing, close the hatch to the loft and walk downstairs to the kitchen.

Georgina will soon need another prescription. I haven't been to the surgery since Kipling passed away because I don't want Jonathan's questions. He'll want to know why the phone doesn't work. He'll want to see Georgina. I open the cupboard under the sink and take out my manual. It's still my thickest file. Angelica has several, but none of them are thicker. I use it to count tablets and measure water, even though I know quantities without looking. I crush the tablets with the back of a teaspoon. When I get upstairs I'll wake Georgina slowly. I'll replace her glass and sit with her until she takes her medication. It could take half an hour. She may do it first time. It depends on how she's feeling. I flick the switch on the kettle and wait for it to boil. I drink tea at the kitchen table. Watch the clock on the oven.

★　★　★

'Good morning,' I whisper, as I unlock the bedroom door and push it open with my hip. 'Rise and shine. Let's get it over and done with.' I close the door behind me, leave the sunlight on the landing. The room smells worse than usual and Georgina has moved. She's not in the position that I left her in last night. Instead she's on her back, her head half-hanging off the bed. Her glass has also moved. It's gone from the bedside table. I always leave it close enough to reach, but now it's on the carpet. A 'V' shape sliced from its side, two single pieces of glass. There is water everywhere. On the bed sheets, the pillows and Georgina's nightdress. It's even on the bible by the bed. The pages are ruined, soaked through to the New Testament. I walk over to Georgina. Her face is white. Her eyes are closed. I place my wrist beneath her nose and wait to feel her breathing. It seems to take forever, but eventually it comes. Slowly and more gentle than it's ever been before. But she is breathing. She is breathing.

Secrets

I'm sitting in the passenger seat of Angelica's car. We're going to see my parents. I have no option. I agreed to it. I've been thinking that it might not be that bad. Angelica can wait in the car. She doesn't need to go in. I'll just sit with my parents for a while, watch television and drink tea. I'll be half an hour and then I'll go back out and tell Angelica that Georgina isn't there. She's gone out for a walk. She didn't say how long she was going to be. Thank you for the trouble, but we've had a wasted journey. We'll take the scenic route back. Chat about the changing weather. Make small talk. It won't be a problem.

We're parked outside Angelica's house and opposite mine. She's forgotten her make-up so has gone back in to get it. I can't stop thinking about Georgina. I want to go back in and redo her room. Plump her pillows. Check her blood pressure again. I look up at her bedroom window, the curtains closed as far as they can go. A thin gap where they don't quite meet. I half expect Georgina to be standing there, looking down at me. Her beautiful eyes. Her lifeless limbs. I look away again. Angelica is coming back. She opens the door and gets in the car. 'Sorry about that,' she says. 'I'd forget my head if it wasn't screwed on.' She puts the key in the ignition and starts the engine at the second attempt. I fasten my seatbelt as we pull away, swerve past the tree in the road and drive out of Cressington Vale.

'Do you know where you're going?' I ask.

'No idea. You'll have to direct me.'

'It's behind the void.'

'What's the void?'

'A pit. The quarry.'

'I didn't know there was a quarry.'

'Are you joking?'

'No. Should I be?'

'Have you not seen the lorries?'

'What lorries?'

'They're always coming and going.'

'No, what are they doing?'

'Coal.'

'What, like a mine?'

'Opencast.'

'Oh right. I'd no idea.'

'I can't believe you've not smelt it.'

'Smells fine to me.'

Angelica turns into the slip road and then the dual carriageway. She has both hands on the steering wheel. She's wearing mittens. Her left hand is pink with yellow polka dots.

Her right hand is yellow with pink polka dots. They look like oven gloves. They must be dangerous to drive in.

'I just need to stop at the garage.'

'Okay.'

'Is that all right?'

'Fine.'

'I need some you-know-whats and some petrol.'

'I'll just stay in the car.'

We pull into the garage and park by the pump nearest the shop. I watch Angelica fill the car with petrol. About half way through the process, she bangs on the window and rolls her woollen fist in the air. I reach over and wind it down an inch.

'Do you want anything?' she says.

'No, I don't think so.'

'What about some flowers?'

'No, it's all right.'

'Come on, you haven't seen her for ages.'

'Do they sell flowers?'

'They sell everything.'

'I don't know.'

'I'll choose some for you.'

'Okay.'

'You can pay me back later.'

I wind the window back up. Angelica returns to the pump and squeezes the trigger. I watch the numbers spin round on the screen. They stop at £9.86. Squeeze again. £9.93. And again. £9.97. Once more. £10.01.

'Bollocks,' she shouts. She bends down and rolls her fist at me again, opens the door before I get chance to lean across. 'Have you got any change?'

'Not on me.'

'Good job I keep a supply then.'

She kneels on the driver's seat, reaches over and opens the glove box. She puts her hand on my knee to help keep her balance. Her coat comes undone at the front. I try not to look at what she's wearing underneath. I focus on the glove box. She takes out a small metal tin. It looks like the one my mother used to keep her pins and needles in. She takes off the lid. It's full of loose change and bracelets. Three gold watches. The time is right on all of them. She picks up a penny.

'I'll be back in a minute.'

'Okay.'

'Put the radio on if you want.'

'I'm fine.'

'Good job, actually. You need the engine running.'

'Why do you need a penny?'

'For the petrol.'

'I thought you were buying flowers and cigarettes.'

'I am.'

'Then you don't need the penny.'

She smiles at me then gets out the car. I watch her walk across the forecourt. She stops halfway, reads the 'coal scum' graffiti and turns around laughing. She points at the words on the wall, nods towards them and mouths something. I give her the thumbs up. I smile at her. I laugh a little. Now I've got both thumbs up. I'm endorsing vandalism. Angelica throws her shoulders back, turns away and continues towards the shop. She returns with a bunch of yellow chrysanthemums for me to give to Georgina. I'll give them to my mother instead. It'll make her day.

* * *

We're two streets away from the house. At least I think we are. I can't remember which turning we need to take. We've been lost twice already. The first time Angelica laughed. The second time she looked in her rear view mirror, pulled over and said, 'Are we even in the right place?' If we get lost again, she'll probably lose her temper. I know she has a temper.

'It's the next left.'

'Are you sure?'

'Yes, it's this one.'

'Haven't we been down here already?'

'No, not yet.'

'All these streets look the same.'

'Left again.'

'We've definitely been here before.'

'It's there, the one with the green door and the glass panel.'

She slows down and pulls up outside the house. It looks smaller than I remember. The front lawn is over a foot high, which means nobody mowed it last summer. Angelica takes her seatbelt off and looks at me. I'm holding the flowers and panicking. This was a bad idea. I should have backed out. I should have come up with a good excuse. Or a bad one even. I should have told Angelica the truth. I wanted to tell her the truth. She'd have understood. We're friends now.

'Are you all right?' she says.

'I'm fine.'

'You look nervous.'

'Do I?'

'You're sweating.'

'I didn't realise.'

'Are you worried about how she'll react?'

'React to what?'

'The news.'

'What news?'

'About Don. I know they were close.'

'Well, it's a lot for her to take in.'

'She'll be glad to get home though, I expect.'

'I suppose so.'

'Now that she's had a bit of a break.'

This is not going to work. My parents are strangers. I haven't spoken to them since Georgina's first stroke. Apart from once when my mother dialled the wrong number. I didn't want their sympathy. My father passing judgment.

'Off you go, then. What are you waiting for?'

I press the button on my seatbelt, loop it over the flowers and pull the handle on the door. Angelica reaches for her handle too. She thinks she's coming with me. She's not coming with me. And I'm not telling her anything. I'll tell her if I absolutely have to. 'Why don't you wait in the car?' She stops, puts her hand back on the steering wheel. 'I'd rather go in on my own.'

'Oh, I see.'

'If you don't mind?'

'No, of course not.'

'I won't be long.'

'It's fine. You go ahead.'

'I'll be half an hour, maximum.'

'I'll just wait here. I've got the radio.'

I cradle the chrysanthemums like I'm

holding a baby, step out of the car and into the cold. I walk to my parents' front door. I can see through the frosted glass. There's a pile of post on the floor. It must have been there for days. I take a deep breath, twist the handle and open the door. It snaps straight back at me. They've got the chain on. I can hear my father's voice. He's telling my mother he heard something. He's telling her to go and find out what it was. I can see the shape of her shoulders through the glass. She's walking towards me. She's opening the door without asking who it is. I could be anyone.

'Hello Mum.' She looks me up and down. She doesn't recognise me. We stand for a few seconds with the door wide open. She's letting the cold in.

'Arthur,' she shouts. 'Arthur, come here.'

My father appears at the end of the hall. He looks at me. Then he looks past me. I turn around. Angelica is waving. Her mouth bright red with lipstick that wasn't there before. My father lifts his hand and holds it in the air for a moment.

'Oh, it's Gordon,' my mother says. I put my hands on her shoulders and step into the house. I kiss her on the cheek and kick the door shut with my heel. I give her a hug and nod at my father. 'What a nice surprise.'

'How are you both?' I say, handing my mother the flowers.

'What's wrong?' says my father.

'Nothing.'

'Oh what wonderful carnations, Gordon.'

'Nothing?'

'No, nothing. They're chrysanthemums, Mum.'

'Well they're lovely, whatever they are.'

'You'd better come in then.'

We walk to the kitchen. I look up at the clock above the fridge. Three minutes past twelve. The table is set for dinner. A loaf of white bread, a family-sized tub of margarine and a jar of my father's pickled onions.

'Do you want a sandwich?' he says.

'No, thank you. I can't stay long.'

'Suit yourself.'

I watch my parents eat and listen to my mother's false teeth. They click in her mouth as she chews her food. They sound like her hip did, before the operation. There's a vase on the windowsill. It has water in it and bits of soil floating on the surface. I walk to the sink, rinse it out and fill it up again. I take the flowers from my mother's lap and put them in the vase. They watch me without speaking.

'Are you well, then?' I say.

'Same as always.'

'Is that good or bad?'

'Neither.'

'What about you, Mum?'

'She's got the runs.'

'Right, I see.'

'Not that there's anything new in that.'

'No?'

'She's up and down like a yo-yo.'

My mother says nothing. She sits and eats her sandwich. My father puts his elbows on the table. It jolts towards him. My mother's plate slides away from her. I bend down and look underneath the table. Only three of its legs touch the floor. There's half an inch gap where the other one hangs in the air.

'Do you still see Georgina?' my mother says. My father looks at her. Then he looks at me. I smile because I think it must be a joke. He looks back at my mother and shakes his head. She stops eating, uses both hands to hold her sandwich. She stares into space and furrows her eyebrows. She's thinking. 'Silly me,' she says.

★   ★   ★

I've been here fifteen minutes. My mother has gone to the living room with a cup of tea and a plate of biscuits. She said she was looking forward to a sit down, even though she's been sitting since I arrived. I'm helping my father clean the dinner plates and cutlery. I wash. He dries. I'm wearing bright yellow Marigolds, like the ones Angelica had in her pockets the day she moved in. I turn the tap and squirt washing-up liquid into the water. It reminds me of Kipling. And Georgina at home.

'Is Mum all right?'

'What do you think?'

'She seems a bit distant.'

'Well, she's old.'

'I know, but . . . '

'What did you expect?'

'Nothing. I've just not seen her for a while.'

'You've not seen either of us.'

'I know. Thanks for the birthday card.'

I wash the pots quicker than he dries them. I put the last fork on the draining board, unplug the sink and reach for the spare tea towel on the worktop. My father uses his towel to slap me across the wrist. I'm suddenly a child again. 'I'm doing them,' he says. 'It's not a race.' I walk to the other side of the kitchen and stand by the door. 'Are you all right, Mum?' I shout, but she doesn't answer me. She probably can't hear me over the television, which is far too loud. I pull a chair up at the table. It's my mother's chair. It has three cushions on the seat so she doesn't have to bend when she sits down.

And to help her stand up again. I watch my father dry the last of the plates. He rubs them with a frown, holds them up to the window and inspects them closely. He checks I've cleaned them right.

'So, who's that then?' he says.

'Who's what?'

'The woman in the car outside.'

'She lives across the road.'

'What's she called?'

'Angelica.'

'What does she do?'

I open my mouth to answer, but nothing comes out. I know when she draws her curtains each morning and when her appointments with the doctor are. I know what clothes she wears and how many miles her car has travelled. I know dates, times and small talk. But I don't know what she does. Not properly. And I don't know what she did. Before she came to Cressington Vale. I know so much about her, yet nothing at all. One thing I'm sure of is that I can hear her voice. She's in my parents' living room. She's talking to my mother.

Note: Dementia = symptoms including confusion, problems with recent memory and emotional problems such as laughing or crying inappropriately. Note end.

'Gordon, this is Angela. She says she came with you.'

'Mum, I thought you put the chain on the door.'

'No, I never put the chain on.'

'It was on when I arrived.'

'Your father puts the chain on.'

'You need to keep it on. Anyone could get in.'

'Charming,' says Angelica.

'Not you. Not like that.'

'I couldn't wait any longer. I'm dying for a piss.'

'Don't say piss.'

'Gordon, would Angela like a sandwich?' says my mother.

'No, Mum. We need to go, I'm afraid. Time to go.'

'You've only just got here,' says Angelica. 'Where's Georgina?'

'She's in bed.'

'At this time?'

'Is she feeling better, Gordon?' says my mother. 'After her little turn?'

'She's just having a nap.'

'Because of the stroke?' says Angelica.

'Is she feeling better Gordon?' says my mother. 'After her little mishap?'

'Yes, because of the stroke. She has to sleep in the afternoon. I should have realised. We'll have to come back another day.'

'Can't you just wake her up?'

'Would you like a biscuit, Angela?' says my mother. 'We've plenty of biscuits.'

'I can't wake her up. Definitely not.'

'Are they chocolate biscuits? You have very nice bone china, Mrs Kingdom.'

'Why thank you, dear. I think they might have nuts in. Do you like nuts?'

'She needs her rest. Really, we need to go.'

'Have you ever had it valued? I need the toilet first.'

'I don't know what you mean, dear. Do you like nuts?' says my mother.

'Fine. You can go to the toilet.'

'Well, thank you very much.'

'There's one under the stairs. Use that one. Don't go upstairs.'

Angelica glares as she walks past me. What in God's name am I doing? Georgina's at home and she's had a third stroke. Not like the others, but still a stroke. I should be with her, not here. I need to step up the routine. More exercises. More noughts and crosses. More everything. I watch Angelica. She doesn't go to the toilet. Instead she goes straight to the front door. She opens it, turns and says, 'Nice to meet you Mrs Kingdom.' Then she walks up the drive and gets back into the car. She puts her seatbelt on and folds her arms. She looks incredibly cross. I look at my father. He's been standing at the end of the hall. He's been listening. 'Anyway, it's been nice to catch up,' I say. But he doesn't reply. He just stares at me, nods at the plaque on the wall. Red with gold lettering: 'We live by faith, not by sight. Two Corinthians. Chapter 5. Verse 7.'

'Does Angela like nuts, Gordon?'

'I don't know, Mum. I really don't know.'

★ ★ ★

Angelica still hasn't started the engine. It's thirty seconds since I kissed my mother, shook my father's hand and came to get in the car. I can see him standing by the curtain in the living room. He's watching us.

'What's going on, Gordon?'

'Nothing.'

'What's wrong with Georgina?'

'Nothing. She's just asleep.'

'You said you hadn't seen her for weeks.'

'I haven't.'

'And you couldn't wake her up?'

'No.'

'Why not?'

'Because of the stroke.'

'I don't believe you.'

This is it. I can't keep my secret any longer.

My father is watching me and he knows that I know that he's watching me. He's not even hiding. He's just standing there. With his cup of tea and his biscuit. And Angelica doesn't believe me. I'll have to tell her everything. She's waiting for an answer. I put my hands in my lap and clasp my fingers together tightly, like I'm about to pray. Like I'm sorry for something.

'It's my mother,' I say. 'She's here to look after my mother.'

'I thought she was sleeping.'

'She is. She needs to rest.'

'Because of the stroke?'

'Because of the stroke.'

Angelica looks at me, sits perfectly still. She pauses for a moment. Then she reaches under the dashboard and twists the key in the ignition. The engine starts first time.

'Let's go,' she says. 'Before I wet myself.'

Temptation

This has to stop. I can't keep my secret any longer. It's half past three in the afternoon and I'm on the chair next to Georgina's bed. The room is nearly dark because the curtains are almost closed. It's raining again. I can hear it beating against the window. It gets louder then softens. Louder then softens. I've been sitting here for over an hour. Listening to its rhythms and counting with my fingers. I've been looking around the room. At the suitcase on top of the wardrobe. At the cobwebs in the corners. At my beautiful bed-ridden wife. And I've been thinking. Making decisions. Georgina's not improving. I know it. She knows it. I don't need my manual and I don't need to carry out tests. I can tell by the look in her eyes, the touch of her hand and the sores on her back. She should have been better by now. She should have been up and walking. But she isn't. And it's my fault. I've taken my eye off the ball. I've been too busy telling lies. But things are going to change. I can't do this on my own. I thought I could. But I can't. The time has come. I need help. Help to change the sheets.

265

Help to move her legs. Help to keep me focused. I'm going to tell Angelica. I'm going to tell her everything. I'm going to tell her tonight. She's my only hope. She always was.

Note: Practice speech. You know what you are doing. You just need someone to help you. It looks much worse than it is. Note end.

It's now been six weeks of Angelica. She was wary at first. She thought me over familiar. She thought I had a way about me that she couldn't put her finger on. She thought I was divorced. I know this because she just told me. She's sitting on the edge of the bed in the spare room, waiting for Benny to paint. He lit his candles twenty minutes ago. But he hasn't started painting. The rain is still heavy and the window is patterned with water and steam from our breathing. It makes it hard to see what he's doing. It makes it hard to see at all. She arrived approximately forty-five minutes ago. She banged on the door, opened the letterbox and shouted for me to let her in. I was in the bedroom with Georgina. I put my hand on her cheek, kissed her forehead and told her that the cavalry was coming. But she didn't hear me speak. She didn't hear the letterbox. So I left her alone, locked her door and made my way downstairs. Angelica went straight to the kitchen, flicked the switch on the kettle and put her handbag on the table. I could smell alcohol on her breath.

It's now half past one in the morning. We've been sitting on the bed together for over a minute. We're waiting for Benny. I'm drinking tea from a mug. Angelica's drinking whiskey from a hip flask. She took it from her bag before we came upstairs. Now she has her feet on the valance. I want to tell her to remove them. They'll make it dirty. But I don't need to. She stands up, walks over to the window and rubs it with her sleeve. She seems agitated. She's wearing a white cotton shirt. It sticks to her forearms.

'I can't believe this fucking rain,' she says. 'I think it's getting worse.'

'It's about the same.'

'Are you sure? I can't see a thing.'

'I'm positive.'

'Well it looks worse to me. Maybe I'm just tired.'

She puts her hand to her mouth as if she's going to yawn but hiccups. I need to tell her about Georgina. I need to tell her before the situation gets any worse. This is the perfect time. I've said I'm going to do it and now I am. I should have done it sooner.

'Angelica, there's something I need to tell you.'

'I don't think he's even there, you know.'

'It's quite important.'

'What's he pissing about at?'

'It's Georgina.'

'Jesus Christ!' She hits the window with the palm of her hand, so hard that it seems to bounce off the glass. If it weren't double glazed, she'd have probably put her fist through. It shocks me into standing.

'What's wrong?'

'Nothing.'

'Nothing?'

'I just can't see that's all.'

'But he's not painting.'

'I know.'

'You'll break the window.' She turns to face me. We are both on our feet, only inches between us. I can smell her breath and perfume. Her face is orange from the glow of the lights in the street. She is close enough to kiss me. She would never kiss me. I wouldn't let her.

'Are you an expert on windows?' She's annoyed with me. How would she like it if I tried to smash her window? She probably wouldn't care. I think she's going to swear at me. I think she's going to leave. But perhaps not. Her shoulders are relaxing. She's shaking her head. She's going to apologise. She smiles and rolls her eyes.

'I'm leaving, Gordon.'

'There's no need to leave. It's only a window. I overreacted.'

'No, I mean I'm moving out.'

'Moving out?'

'Yes.'

'You can't move out.'

'I'm going back to my husband. We're giving it another go.'

'You only just moved in.'

'He says he can forgive me.'

'Can he?'

'Yes.'

'I didn't know you'd done anything wrong.'

'I didn't. Not really. He thought I'd had an affair.'

'Did you?'

'I'm sorry about losing my temper.'

'Did you have an affair?'

'I guess I'm on edge about it all. I'm just tired. It's all the late nights.'

'But did you have an affair?'

'Of course not. It doesn't matter now. What were you trying to tell me?'

'Sorry?'

'You said you wanted to tell me something.'

'Oh, nothing.'

'Go on.'

'It's nothing.'

'You said something about Georgina'

'No I didn't.'

'Yes you did. Is she all right?'

'She's fine.'

'Is she finally coming home?'

'No.'

'No?'

'I mean yes. Not for long.'

'Is there a problem?'

'She loved her flowers. Did I tell you she loved her flowers?'

'No, I don't think you did.'

'Well she did, she loved them.'

'Okay. I'm glad.'

'That was it. Georgina loved her flowers.'

The cavalry has vanished. After all my preparation. I feel faint. I have to put my hand on the wall to stop myself from falling. I sit back down on the bed. Angelica turns to the window and rubs the glass with her sleeve. I look at the space where my files used to be. An empty bookcase gathering dust. She puts her hands on her hips and hiccups again. Benny has started painting. I need another cup of tea.

'Where are you going?' she says.

'I'm making a drink. Do you want one?'

'Water, please. It might get rid of my hiccups.'

I take a glass from the cupboard and run it under the tap to wash the dust out. I fill it with cold water and place it on the worktop. I put the kettle on to boil, sit down at the table and wait. It's almost two o'clock in the morning. I've been watching Benny for months so I'm used to the late nights. But tonight I'm tired. In fact, I'm exhausted. And now Angelica is leaving. She's been here six weeks and I have several files' worth of notes on her. I've bought her gifts and she's met my parents. Right now, she's the only person who can help me. But she won't be here to do it. She'll go when she's still needed.

The kettle boils. As I stand up, I notice Angelica's handbag. It's pink like her slippers. And she's left it unzipped. I could put my hand in. I could open it and look inside. She'd never know. I put a teabag in a mug. There are two bottles of milk in the fridge. One of them is full, the other almost empty. I take the bottle that's already been opened and check the label. I look back at the bag. It's almost like she's left it there on purpose. Like she wants me to look. The rain has eased or the wind died down. It's definitely quieter. If she comes downstairs I'll hear her footsteps. I finish making tea and put the mug next to the glass of water on the worktop. There's a notepad in the cupboard under the sink. It's for emergencies. This is an emergency. I take it out and grab a pen from the cutlery drawer. I walk over to the table, put my hand in Angelica's bag and start taking things out.

Note: Angelica's inventory = Tissues. Nail polish (three colours). Make-up. Mirror. Photo Album. Swiss army knife. Note end.

I put the items on the table. The bag is huge. I thought there'd be more in it. The photo album has a red cover and the word 'Love' printed across the top in gold lettering. I open it carefully. My fingers shaking. It holds two photos. One is of a man around my age. He has a moustache and is standing beside a boat. It was taken during summer. Or in another country. The other photo is of a boy, except he doesn't look like a boy. He looks like a man. It's a school photograph and he's sitting in front of a blue background with books painted on for effect. It could've been taken anywhere. He has a wide smile and dark hair. I've seen him before. In Angelica's kitchen. He looks exactly like her.

I've been downstairs for almost nine minutes. Angelica's hiccups might have gone by now. I should go back up. If I tell her about Georgina, she might change her mind about leaving. She'll feel guilty and stay. One by one I put the items back into the bag. Apart from the purse, which is leather and has the letter 'A' stitched into the side. It looks almost new. Slowly, I undo the clasp. My tea is going cold. She'll be wondering where I am. The purse is full of notes, but no cards. I take them out, lick my thumb and count them. Two hundred and forty pounds. Ten twenties. Three tens. Two fives. I fold the notes and put them back in the purse. There is a zipped compartment sewn into the lining of the bag. I pull the zip and put my fingers inside. I can feel one object. It is long and round. I take it out and put it on the table. A thick, black marker pen. I stare at it for a while. A minute. Maybe two. Then I place it back inside the purse. There must be some mistake.

★ ★ ★

Benny has extinguished his candles and Angelica is asleep on the bed in the darkness. Her hair lies loose across her cheek and her feet are under the covers. The hip flask is on the floor. I put our drinks on the bookcase. Second shelf down from the top. I need to

273

wake her. This is where I sleep. 'Angelica,' I whisper. No response. I bend my back, lean closer. 'Angelica, you've fallen asleep.' Again, nothing. It must be the drink. I raise my voice a little, 'I've brought your water. How are the hiccups?' She doesn't answer. She lies there motionless. Her chest isn't moving. I put my fingers to her wrist and check her pulse out of habit. She's alive. Of course she's alive. I shake her gently by the shoulder. I speak at my normal volume, 'Angelica, it's gone two o'clock. You can't sleep here.' Her fingers twitch.

'David, I'm fine,' she says softly, without waking. I look around for a notepad, but they're all in the loft. Or under the kitchen sink. I don't really need one anyway. I can remember a name.

'Angelica?' Back to nothing. 'Angelica?' She's not going anywhere. She'll have to stay here. I could sleep on the sofa and use the spare sheets from the airing cupboard. They should be warm enough. I'll wake her early and ask her downstairs for breakfast. Tea and toast for two. It's Valentine's Day tomorrow. I can give her the card I've made. My way of saying thank you. That's all. She'll be polite and appreciative. Then we'll sit at the table and talk. I'll ask her about the marker pen. She'll explain everything. Then she'll say she's sorry for falling asleep. That she can't believe how tired she must've been. And I'll say it's fine, no bother at all. Then we'll be quiet and struggle for something to say. Until she asks about Georgina. Then I'll crack a joke. And we'll laugh together. But she'll ask me again. And I'll tell her the truth. She'll completely understand. She'll change her mind about leaving.

I reach across the bed and pull the covers over her. She doesn't flinch or make a sound. I stand up straight, look out at the street and see Benny. He's standing by his window, looking in my direction with his hands in the air. He holds them in front of his face with thumbs and index fingers touching each other. They make a shape. An oval, like an egg or an eye. Can he see me? I'm in darkness, but I haven't been paying attention. I haven't been hiding. I stay perfectly still and look back. We're two shadows, our eyes alert and adjusted. I could stand here like this until he moves. I could signal to him. Or I could pretend that nothing's happening. I could reach across and pull the curtain. Calm and casual. I've not done anything wrong. Unless he saw Angelica. Then he'll be suspicious. I can hear her breathing heavily behind me. I raise my arms and pretend to stretch. I walk to the window, look down at the puddles on the road and up at the clouds in the sky. They are deep blue and black, like a swirling bruise. But I don't look back at Benny. I simply close the curtains. Leave him outside with the night.

Umbrage

It's ten past five in the morning. I'm sitting on the chair next to Georgina's bed. If it were spring or summer, it would be light outside. But it isn't. It's dark and starless. Like the night we got trapped by the tide, less than two years ago. We'd gone away for the weekend. For Georgina's birthday. It was my treat. We stayed by the coast and walked along the cliff top both days before dinner. The wind made it cold, but the view was worth it. We had a wonderful time. That afternoon was colder than most. We wore gloves and held hands, our 'jackets in packets' zipped tight around our necks. The sea was rough and empty. We reached the end of the bridleway and stopped for tea in a café by the beach. We were the only ones in there. Georgina ate a scone filled with cream and jam. I burnt my tongue. I remember her laughing.

We decided to walk back along the sand. We'd done it before without problems, though it had been earlier then, when the tide was still way out. This time the tide was much closer. I said I thought we should hurry, but

Georgina insisted we'd be fine. She told me I worried too much. I needed to relax. Enjoy it. But she was wrong, because halfway along the beach, maybe a mile, I realised we weren't going to make it. We'd left it too late and the tide was coming in. I began to panic, grabbed Georgina's hand and started to run. We ran together, breathing heavily and stopping to walk every fifty yards or so. Then running again. Georgina laughed and screamed between breaths. Like she hadn't a care in the world. We must've looked ridiculous. We must've looked like children. And we nearly made it too. But we didn't. The sea beat us back to the shore and we had to wade the last stretch in our trousers. Our shoes soaked to the core. Our feet freezing cold. That evening we shared a bath and watched the day turn to night through the skylight. We laughed together. The sky full of clouds. Dark and starless.

★　★　★

It's Valentine's Day tomorrow. I've made them a card each. One for Georgina and one for Angelica. I found Georgina's old school box in the loft last week. It was full of felt tip pens. Coloured card. Glitter and glue. She used to make all sorts of things. Sparkling certificates. Milk carton robots. Puppets out of my old socks. She'd use them in her lessons and give them away to the best-behaved children. Any excuse to come home and make something else. She loved being a teacher, even when she became Head. In fact, she loved it more. She said she felt like she could make a difference. I did my best to support her, even though I found it difficult. She always had to work late. She always went to meetings. She always earned more money.

I made Angelica's card from pink paper and stuck a collage of flowers on the front. I cut pictures out of magazines. The message inside says, 'Best wishes. Gordon.' If I wrote it again I'd write it with a marker pen. Just to see her reaction. Georgina's card is white with a red heart. Two stick people holding hands. I used a compass to draw the outline of their heads. Inside, it says, 'Happy Valentine's Day. Get well soon. With love, G.' I also made a card for me, from her. It was more of a postcard. A photograph of Kipling with Georgina. Don Donald took it more than ten years ago. I stuck it to a piece of paper, cut around its edges and wrote on the back, 'Happy Valentine's Day. Love from you know who.' That's what she would've written, if she were able. I made them last week, when she was getting better.

I straighten my back in the chair by the bed and look at Georgina now, confined to this room. Her life taken without warning. My life too. Our life together. If I think about it long enough I start to get resentful. I start to blame Georgina. She could have done something differently. Spent less time at work. Spent more time with me. Even now, watching her sleeping, her eyes closed, her face void of colour, it's hard to understand. I shuffle slowly to the edge of the chair and put my hand on her shoulder. 'Wake up,' I whisper gently. 'Please wake up.' But she can't provide a response. There's nothing she can do. It's not her fault. I know it's not her fault. I sit back on the seat and rub my eyes with my fists. I think about Angelica. Her eyes closed. Her mouth wide open. Asleep in our spare room.

Valentine

I'm lying on the floor at the end of Georgina's bed. The room is lit by sunlight pouring through the gap in the curtains. I can feel the heat on my cheeks and smell Georgina's dressing gown. I used it last night as a pillow. This is the first time we've woken up in the same room since she had her first stroke. It feels warm and familiar. If I listen hard I'll hear birds in trees and voices outside in the street. Noises downstairs in the kitchen. The sound of cupboards closing. Cutlery rattling in dishes. Angelica. I open my eyes and get to my feet. Georgina hasn't moved. She's in the same position as before, when I kissed her goodnight and set up my bed. She looks dreadful in the sunlight. I can hear the kitchen door. The stairs are creaking. I stand by Georgina and hold the back of my hand to her forehead. Her temperature is through the roof. I pick up the glass from the dresser, dip my fingers into the water and touch her cheeks to cool her down. Angelica knocks on the door. She's brought me breakfast in bed.

'Gordon?'

'Hold on. I'll just be a minute.'
'Breakfast.'
'I'll be out in a second.'
'Why are you whispering?'
'I'm not.'
'Are you all right?'
'I'm fine.'
'You don't sound fine.'
'I'm just getting dressed. I'm nearly done.'
'Are you decent?'
'Sort of.'
'Then I'm coming in.'
'Don't come in.'
'I'm coming in. Your tea's going cold.'
'Angelica.'
'I've seen it all before.'
'Please, Jesus, don't come in.'

I watch the handle turning. There's no need to panic. The door is locked. She'll have to wait outside. I'll ignore her. I'll wait for her to go back downstairs and then I'll go and join her. The handle's still turning. She can get in. The door's opening. I didn't lock it. I came back from the bathroom, made my bed and fell asleep. She's coming in. This is what I wanted. She can help us. I grab Georgina's hand and grip it tight. My fingertips are wet like her cheeks, but her eyes are closed. It looks like she's been crying in her sleep. Angelica steps into the room. She is holding a plastic tray with tea and toast on it. Breakfast with Angelica. She looks at me, then at Georgina. Her mouth falls open in horror. The tray slides out of her hands. It crashes to the floor.

We stand in silence. She says nothing. I say nothing.

We stand and we stare.

At each other.

At my wife.

★   ★   ★

'She needs to go to hospital, Gordon.' Fifteen minutes have passed since Angelica found Georgina and we're standing in the kitchen. I've cleaned the bedroom carpet, soaked up the milk with kitchen towel and made two fresh cups of tea.

'No, she doesn't. She's fine.'

'She doesn't look fine.'

'Everything's under control.'

'I don't believe you.'

'I'm looking after her.'

'How?'

'With the manual.'

Angelica puts her hands to her head and starts pacing back and forth. Her fingers are shaking. She has nothing to worry about. I know what I'm doing. She can't be angry because I've done nothing wrong. She looks at the clock on the wall. She hasn't touched her tea yet.

'When did it happen?'

'Six weeks ago. The day before you moved in.'

'Jesus Christ, Gordon.'

'And maybe again this week. She'd been getting better.'

'I could smell it. I knew there was something.'

'What do you mean?'

'Illness. Something not quite right'

'I bathe her every day.'

'It's not the same.'

'It's the best I can do.'

I turn away from her. Now I'm shaking too. I look through the window. The sunlight creeps over the house and into the back garden. It forms a triangle in the corner of the lawn. The rest is still in shade. Coated in frost.

'She needs to go to hospital, Gordon.'

'She doesn't, she'll get better.'

'How do you know that? You can't do this.'

'I am doing it and I've done it before.'

'Not like this though. Not on your own.'

'I want you to help me.'

'You're killing her.'

'Help me.'

'I can't, Gordon.'

'Why not?'

'I wouldn't know what to do.'

'I'll show you.'

'I don't want you to show me.' She stops pacing, throws her arms in the air and stares straight at me. She looks ready to explode.

'I thought you'd understand.'

'You lied to me, Gordon. I took you to your parents' house.'

'I thought we were friends.'

'We hardly know each other.'

'What about Benny?'

'What about him?'

'We watch Benny together.' I watch Angelica lower her arms. Then I look at the floor. I cover my eyes with my hand and squeeze my brow with my fingers. I'm pretending to cry, but I don't know what it feels like. I can't remember. It seems so long ago. This is me upset. She'll never believe it.

'You need to ring the hospital. They'll send an ambulance.'

'I can't.'

'You have to. Georgina needs help.'

'She's getting help.'

'She needs real help.'

'You don't understand. We've done this before and we know what we're doing. You can help us.'

'Gordon, she seems barely conscious.'

'It's just a setback. She's been getting better.'

'I can't help you, Gordon. She needs professional help.'

I bring my fist down on the kitchen worktop. It makes the sink and the plates in the cupboards rattle. It stops us both. I've never done it before. Angelica backs away from me. She's got no idea what we've been through. All she does is drink my tea and stare out of the window. My window. I want to ask her about the marker pen. Where did she get it from? What about the footballs in the garden? It should be me who's asking the questions. Demanding explanations. Losing my temper.

'No, she doesn't. No-one needs to know.'

'What's your fucking problem?' she says. 'You're insane.'

'Don't swear.'

'Do you want her to die?'

'You're always swearing.'

'Can you live with the guilt?'

'There's nothing to feel guilty about.'

'She's not getting better, Gordon.'

'She will get better.'

'Not like this.'

'It's what she wanted.'

'You don't know that.'

'Yes I do.'

'How?'

'She told me. We have a system.'

I open the cupboard under the sink and take out my manual. It seems thicker than ever. Angelica watches me. We've raised our voices. She's louder than me. Taller than me. Pacing up and down. Georgina must have heard us. We've woken her up. She's lying in bed, feeling for her water and wondering where I am.

'Gordon, calm down,' says Angelica. 'I'm sorry. I'm still in shock.'

I walk to the table, pull out a chair and sit down. I open my manual and cover my eyes again. I squeeze my brow with my fingers. Drag them over my eyes. Still pretending to cry. This time my hands are wet. There are tears on my cheeks and my chin and they are falling onto the table. Angelica walks towards me. She puts her hand on my shoulder. On the back of my neck. Pulling me close. She wraps her arms around my head and holds it to her stomach. I grip the manual with one hand and her leg with the other. I hold it tight below the knee. For dear life and comfort.

'This is what she wanted.'

'I have to go, Gordon.'

'Don't go.'

'I have to. I need to take this in. I'll come back later on.'

'We haven't had breakfast.'

'I'm meeting Michael.'

'Who's Michael?'

'He's my husband.'

Vicious circle

Georgina likes her card. I gave it to her this morning when Angelica had gone. I sat on the chair by the bed and opened the envelope. She was wide-awake. Her eyes were fully open. I took out the card and held it up for her to look at. I pointed to Kipling and squeezed her hand. 'Do you like it?' I said. One small, fragile stroke = Yes. 'Did you hear any noises earlier?' One pinch, barely noticeable = No. I held the glass of water to her lips. She slowly let some slip into her mouth. She managed three sips. Then she started coughing. I put my hand on her back and tried to help her straighten, but it didn't seem to help. The coughing got worse before it eased. After more than thirty seconds, it stopped. I held Georgina's head and lowered it back onto the pillow. She was breathing quickly, but the danger had passed. I talked about the weather until her eyes closed and she drifted into sleep. Her breathing returned to normal. I walked to the opposite side of the room and placed her card on the dressing table. Then I opened mine and stood them together.

Note. Tear Angelica's card into strips. Cut strips into squares. Note end.

I'm in the kitchen baking carrot cake. I've turned on the oven, prepared the tin and grated the carrots. The rest of the ingredients are spread out across the worktop, on plates and in mugs. One by one, I put them into the mixing bowl, adding eggs, beating well. I fold the mixture until my fingers ache. Then I pour it into the tin, smooth it with the back of a spoon and open the oven door. The heat rolls out, warms my skin and burns my lips. I slide the cake onto a shelf. I look up at the clock and make a note of the time. Three fifteen. More than six hours since Angelica found Georgina. She hasn't been back yet. Everything is normal. Nothing has changed. I expected her to phone the hospital, describe what she saw and tell them to send out an ambulance. I've been waiting by the window, listening for sirens, expecting Doctor Jonathan. But it hasn't happened. Georgina's still upstairs and she has no idea that someone else has seen her. I haven't said a word. It would break her heart.

It's time to make the topping for the carrot cake. I take a bowl from the worktop and put in some cream cheese and icing sugar. I add the juice of half an orange, squeeze and stir together. When I've finished, I'm going to create a new schedule. I'm going to work twice as hard and Georgina is going to get better. She's not in any pain and she's still able to swallow. Things might start to change. She might begin to talk again. She might be walking in a month. Angelica is going to change her mind. That's why there's no ambulance. She's been thinking about it. She's going to help me. Her husband too. We can lift Georgina together. We'll take a side each and move her into a chair. So she feels normal again, at least for a while. I finish stirring the mixture. The cake smells delicious.

★ ★ ★

It's midnight. I'm waiting for Angelica. Half an hour ago she pulled back her curtain, looked over at the house and up at the spare room. She was looking for me, but I wasn't there. I was with Georgina, peering through the gap in the curtains. Now I'm in the spare room and Angelica is coming. We're going to watch Benny. She's going to apologise and tell me I was right. I know what I'm doing because I've done it before. Here she is. She's opening her front door and walking across the road. She wraps her arms around her chest and skips up and onto the pavement. Then she stops, looks up at the window. I smile at her and wave, but she doesn't smile back. Or wave. Instead she looks away and continues across the road. I take a single step backwards. A deep breath. I check Georgina's door is locked and make my way downstairs. The letterbox rattles. There's a note on the floor in the hall. I pick it up, open the door and watch Angelica running back across the street. I go to shout, but she's almost home and I don't know what to say. She opens her door and disappears inside the house. I take the note to the kitchen. The words are gold and written in capital letters. They're difficult to read. I hold the paper to the light.

'GET HELP. IF YOU DON'T, I WILL'

I sit down at the table and read the note again out loud. Angelica is threatening me. She hasn't changed her mind. She was never going to help us. I stand up and walk to the kitchen window. The sky is clear and the stars are out. My heart is racing and my throat is dry. I pour myself a glass of water and drink it in one. I need to calm down. There's no need to panic. She clearly hasn't thought things through. She doesn't understand.

I pick up the note and walk to the living room window. I look across the street at Angelica's house. It's in total darkness. She's pretending to be asleep. She wants me to think that she's gone to bed and that there's no point trying to reason with her. I pull back the curtain and take my pen from the windowsill. The wind is blowing through the trees on Cressington Vale. The branches move against the stillness of the stars. I walk to the hall and put my coat on. I wrap it tight around my shoulders and lift the collar up and over the back of my neck. My gloves are in the pockets. I take them out and squeeze my fingers inside. I pick up my keys, open the door and step out into the night. There's still no sign of life in Angelica's house. It doesn't matter. We don't need to talk. Not tonight.

I walk to the end of the garden, open the gate and cross the road. It's extremely quiet and incredibly still. There are lights in houses, but not many. I stand outside Angelica's door and hold the note up to the moonlight. I read her words for one last time. Then I turn the paper over and write some words of my own. In normal letters, not capitals: 'Help us, or I'll tell him everything.' I fold the note and push it through the letterbox. I turn and walk back across the street, into the house and to the kitchen. I take my coat off and flick the switch on the kettle. I make myself a cup of tea.

Windows

'We'll have to come back tomorrow,' said Georgina. She reached across and put her hand on my knee. We were driving home from her mother's house after spending the day cleaning, clearing and throwing things away. Furniture, books and jewellery. Ornaments, clothes and cutlery. Everything she owned. Georgina said that we weren't throwing things away, we were simply deciding not to keep them. It made her feel less guilty. The house had to go on the market. We had no choice.

'I'll ask Don about the freezer. He says he needs a new one.'

'That's fine. We don't need it.'

'And the lawnmower. He might want that as well.'

'Really?'

'We don't need it.'

'Fine. He can have it.'

We pulled up at the traffic lights. The last lights before the entrance to Cressington Vale. We sat and listened to the rain and the window wipers scraping back and forth across the windscreen. I looked in the rear view mirror at the photos on the parcel shelf. We'd found them just before we left the house, stashed away in one of the kitchen cupboards, a plastic shopping bag hidden behind packets of cereal, all out of date except one. The photos were of my father. Various poses in various places. Him on a beach with an ice cream. Him at a zoo with a monkey. Him in a car park, waving with one hand and eating a sandwich with the other. There were fifteen photos and in every one he was wearing his dancing suit and shoes. In every one he was smiling.

'What shall we do with them?' I said. Georgina sighed and took her hand from my knee. She pulled the sun visor down and looked in the mirror. She adjusted her hair and sighed.

'I don't know Gordon.'

'We need to do something. We can't keep them.'

'Then why don't you get rid of them?'

'How?'

'I don't know. Bin them. Burn them. Whatever makes you feel better.'

Georgina flipped the visor back to the roof of the car and turned away from me. The lights changed from red to amber, amber to green. We drove into Cressington Vale, swerved around the tree and pulled up outside the house. I turned off the engine. It was early evening. The sky was neither blue nor black.

'There's so much that I don't know,' I said. Georgina sighed again, shook her head and climbed out of the car. She hitched her skirt and stretched her back. 'You can't know everything, Gordon,' she said. 'No-one ever does.'

★　★　★

It's half past nine in the morning and I'm sitting in the backseat of a taxi. Georgina is at home alone. This morning I sat with her and ate my breakfast. I handed her a yoghurt and she refused to take it. I peeled back the lid, scooped some out with a spoon and put it to her mouth. She slowly turned her head away. I asked her what the matter was. Would she try something else? But she didn't speak to me. She wouldn't even try. Her face was pale. Her pulse was slow. She still looked awful. And now I'm here and the meter is running. I've never been in a taxi before. It's always seemed like such a waste of money.

'Who lives here then?' says the driver. He is twenty-four-years-old and engaged to an eighteen-year-old girl who has a six-month old child called Melissa. He is not Melissa's father. But he knows her father because they went to school together. The pink paint on his overalls is from decorating Melissa's nursery, which is currently blue. He will be a taxi driver until something better comes along. He refuses to work on the lorries. He hasn't told me his name.

'My mother and father live here.'

'Really?'

'Yes.'

'They must be old.'

'Yes. I suppose they are.'

I've decided to speak to my parents and ask for their help. There is no-one else to turn to. No other family. No friends. I wish Don Donald were here. I wish I hadn't spoken to him like I did. He would've sat at the kitchen table, drank tea and helped me make decisions. We'd have been a partnership. But Don is gone. And I am here. Outside my parents' house again. My fingers trembling. From the nerves and the memories. The taxi meter running.

'Are you going in? It's getting expensive.'

'Not yet.'

'Okay. No problem.'

'Thank you.'

'I haven't got all day though.'

'I'll just be a minute.'

I take a deep breath. This is what will

happen. I'll pay the driver and ask him to come back in half an hour. Then I'll walk to the front door, knock and wait for my mother to answer, just like she did when I came with Angelica. I will hear my father shout in the background. My mother will let me into the house and I will kiss her on the cheek. I'll say hello to them both. She'll be pleased to see me. He'll be polite, suspicious and offer me a drink. We'll walk to the kitchen together. I'll look at the plaque on the wall. We live by faith, not by sight.

'Back again?' my father will ask as he fills the kettle with water. 'What did we do to deserve this?' I'll smile and pretend he's being nice. But both of us will know that he's not. It will be awkward. Painful. We'll wait for the kettle to boil and its spluttering and hissing will fill the silence between us. Then he'll pour the tea. I'll ask him to sit down.

'Dad, I've got something to tell you,' I'll say. 'It's important.'

'Right. Okay then.'

'And you need to listen carefully, because it isn't easy for me.'

'All right. I'm listening. But before you start, there's no money. Nothing.'

'It isn't that. I don't want any money.'

'What do you want?'

'Your help. It's Georgina. She's had

another stroke. She's extremely ill. I don't know what to do.'

'Is she outside in the car?'

'No. She's at home. She's been in bed since it happened and no-one knows. I've been caring for her myself. I have all the notes. All the information. But she's not getting any better. She was. But now she isn't.'

My father will say nothing, at first. He will fidget in his seat, raise his eyebrows and scratch the tip of his nose. It will mean that he is thinking. Taking it in. Absorbing the information and preparing a response.

'What does Doctor Richmoor say?'

'He doesn't know about it either. He moved to New Zealand before Christmas.'

'Really? I didn't know that.'

'Dad, she's dying.'

'New Zealand? That's a long way.'

I will begin to regret my decision to come here. My father has never taken me seriously. Why should he now? I'm fifty-two-years-old. He's got better things to worry about. Like his guilty conscience and my mother's health. I will start again.

'It happened on my birthday. Everything was fine and then it just happened. We'd been doing everything right. Just like they'd told us. She'd been getting better.'

'Why didn't you take her to hospital?'

'I panicked. It wasn't as bad as the first time. I thought we could do it alone. Without all the hassle. All the interfering. I couldn't face it again.'

'So you haven't told anyone?'

'No. I have it all written down. I know what I'm doing.'

'Do you?'

'Yes. All we need is an extra pair of hands.'

'You don't need me, Gordon.'

'I do. You can help me lift her.'

'I'm an old man.'

'So am I, Dad. So am I.'

My father will stand up, turn and face the window. I will notice the shape of his shoulders, crooked and altered by age. And I will wait for him to speak. Some words of advice. Anything. But nothing will come. So I'll do the talking instead. I'll tell him it's okay. I understand. When I get home, I'll phone the hospital. They'll know what to do. 'It's for the best,' he'll say. And then we'll change the subject. Talk about something different. The weather. New Zealand. And then the deafening silence.

'I'd better get going.' I'll walk back down the hall and into the living room. My father will follow and watch me kiss my mother on the cheek. She'll barely know it's happening. I'll smile at her. Then I'll walk to the front door and step outside. My father will clear his throat.

'You need to put an end to it,' he'll say. 'You need to call it off.' I'll stand my ground. Look him straight in the eye.

'I don't know what you mean.'

'Angela. That woman.'

He will say it like he's speaking to a teenager. It will upset me. His lack of compassion. His inability to empathise. I will want to grab him by the collar. This elderly man. I'll want to shake him and shake him, unleash sentence after bottled-up sentence, line after carefully prepared line. Rehearsed over decades. But I won't do it. I will never do it. I will turn and walk away.

Note: *This is what you should have said. I'm sorry that this has happened. It's not your fault. I'm here for you. Note end.*

'Are you going in, then?'

I am still in the taxi. The driver has lit a cigarette and wound down the window. He rests his elbow on the glass and flicks ash on the road with his fingers. He tips back his head and holds the cigarette tight between his lips. It sounds like a kiss on release.

'No. We can go.'

'Are you sure?'

301

'Yes.'

'Where to?'

'Home.'

'Well that was a waste of time.'

We don't speak again until the car arrives on Cressington Vale. I ask him to stop in the same place he picked me up. At the end of the street. Nowhere near the house. I pay him, say thank you and pull my coat around my ears. He reverses back onto the main road via the pavement and drives away. Exhaust smoke follows the car and hangs in the air. It rises slowly, like lifting fog. When I get home I check on Georgina. I've been gone for less than an hour. Nothing has changed. Everything remains.

I walk downstairs to the kitchen and open the cupboard under the sink. I pick up my manual and place it on the table. A failed document. Useless information. My recipes are on the worktop. They're held together with more than twenty staples, each lined up down the side, one by one with no gaps. I lick my thumb and flick through them. Fruit cake. Chocolate cake. Angel cake. Perfect. I take a teaspoon from the cutlery drawer and use it to mark the page. A narrow band of sunlight bisects the paper horizontally. Ingredients in one half. Instructions in the other. I follow the light to the sink, turn on the tap, rinse my hands, hold them to my chest and rub them together. I look up and out of the window. Benny is in the garden. He has a football under his arm. It has four squares on it, drawn on with marker pen. They look like a puzzle. Or a window. I stop rubbing my hands. Water runs from my fingertips to my wrists and forearms. It forms a stream that ends at my elbows and falls away to the floor. I stare at Benny. He stares back. His cover blown. He must have thought I was out. He didn't see the taxi. The badges on his lapel are three different shapes and colours. One red triangle. One blue square. One yellow circle.

'Get out of my garden.' He can't hear me, so I repeat the words. 'Get out of my garden.' The sun moves behind a cloud and the strip of light evaporates. Benny squints and arches his neck. He tries to read my lips. 'Get out of my garden. Get out of my garden. Get out of my garden.' The tap is running and the sound of the water hitting the metal floor of the sink rings constant. It's the backdrop to my panicking. I lower my hands and walk towards the door. By the time I open it and step outside, Benny is halfway up and over the wall. His arms and legs flailing, desperate to get out of the garden. I watch him climb and disappear, listen to the rustle and snap of bushes and branches being stamped on. The sound of Benny running away. Like a teenage boy.

Watershed

It's been two days since we exchanged notes. Angelica hasn't been back. Late last night her husband arrived. I recognised him from the photograph I found in her bag. His car pulled up outside the house. Its lights dipped then disappeared. I've seen it here before. It's the car I saw before Judy broke in. He stepped out and onto the road, pulled his sleeve back and looked at his watch, bent to check his haircut in the wing mirror. He looked like he did in the picture. Apart from the moustache. He looks younger without it. I watched him walk to the house, knock once on the door and enter without waiting. He reappeared at the living room window and pointed at the car. Its lights flashed twice. Less than twenty minutes later, the house was in darkness. I made a note and opened a new file. M is for Michael (Angelica's husband).

This morning it snowed again. A thin veil of white across the street. I stood at the spare room window. John Bonsall was wearing his rubber suit and shovelling the snow from his drive. He made a path from the door to the pavement. A perfect curve around the lawn.

When he'd finished, he walked to the middle of the road and started clearing the rest of the street. He does it on purpose. Always being kind. Always being neighbourly. He shovelled a path along the pavement to Ina Macaukey's house, then another to Angelica's. He even cleared a trail from the pavement to their doors. The snow reappeared as quick as he removed it. It was a pointless task. Like pleating fog. But he kept on going anyway. All the way to Don's house. He came back two hours later, did it all again.

Angelica's husband left this afternoon. I'd fallen asleep in the kitchen with my head on the table and my fingers round the handle of my mug. I woke to the sound of his car engine starting. I stood up slowly, poured my tea in the sink and walked to the window in the living room. I watched him drive forward, reverse, then drive forward again. Up and out of the street. A three-point turn in the falling snow. It left a car-shaped space on the road. A temporary tarmac island. I looked across at the house. Angelica's curtains were closed. A single vase of flowers on the windowsill. Trapped between the fabric and the glass. Three red, two white and several yet to bloom.

Note: Husband arrives — 23:47. Flowers appear — 23:54. Lights out — 00:03. Carnations, lilies and freesia. Not one rose. Note end.

It's now eight o'clock in the evening. I'm sitting with Georgina and eating a sandwich. She's been awake for twenty minutes. I've been telling her about the snow outside. The way it's been reflecting the sun. Brightening the street. Like it did during our first winter on Cressington Vale. When Don built that snowman and she helped him roll it. 'Can you remember?' I said. But she didn't answer. She just listened to me talking. Watched me treading water. I took a bite from my sandwich and put the plate on the bedside table. Georgina hasn't eaten all day. Every time I ask her if she wants something, she says she isn't hungry. I reach into my pocket and take out a packet of strawberry-flavoured jelly cubes. They should melt in her mouth and slip down her throat. I break one in half and put it to her lips. 'You need to eat,' I say. But she refuses. She keeps her mouth shut. Tries spitting on my fingers. I stand up, pull my handkerchief out of my sleeve and wipe saliva from her chin.

'Georgina.' That's all I can say. Nothing else. Just her name. I stand up and over her.

307

She looks angry, frightened and barely alive. I watch her try to lift her head, but she doesn't have the strength. 'Here, let me help you.' I put my hand on the back of her neck and raise her gently. I rearrange her pillows, but she reaches out and stops me. She holds me by the wrist. Her grip is weak. I can barely feel it. 'What's the matter?' I say. 'Too many?' She let's go. Holds my hand and strokes my palm. 'Yes? No problem.' I take a pillow from under her head and place it on my lap. 'Is that better?' I ask. She doesn't need to answer. It's not better. It never will be. I can see it in her eyes. She looks up at me and slowly reaches over. She gathers all the strength she has to drag the pillow back onto the bed, wrap her arm around it, smother her face, stop herself from breathing. I should intervene immediately. Instead I watch her struggle. I think about closing my eyes. Pretending not to notice. Then I lean over, remove the pillow and hold her hand. I cry once she's fallen asleep.

X-rated

This morning I made a decision. I'm going to threaten Angelica. She's been here for seven weeks and I've been nothing but hospitable. I've made her cakes and bought her gifts. She's drunk my tea and used my toilet. Now it's time for her to do something for me. Something for us. I'm tired of waiting. She's not going to change her mind about helping and she's not going to phone for an ambulance. But I have no choice. She's all I've got. It's time for me to take action.

It's half past eleven on Saturday morning and I'm standing in my front garden pretending to dig. Any minute now Angelica is going to leave the house to go to the newsagents. When she does I'm going to call her over and confront her. I'll confront her husband too if necessary. His car is blocking Don Donald's drive. It sticks out like a sore thumb against the others on the street. It's an eyesore. Water drips from the mudguards onto the road and yet it hasn't rained all morning. He must've put it through a car wash. He's trying to impress her. I want to introduce myself. Welcome him to Cressington Vale. He'll know who I am. Angelica will have mentioned me by now. This is Gordon, she'll say, the man I told you about. The one who bought me the pornography. The one whose dog committed suicide. The one who's slowly killing his wife. I bet that's what she's said. None of it's the truth.

Here they are. They're leaving the house. Him first and Angelica behind. She stops to lock the door. I watch from the garden and think about what I'm going to say. She's wearing high heel shoes and a skirt that finishes above her knee. It's far too young for her. She's forty-two-years-old and dressed like a schoolgirl. Her husband walks to the end of the drive and stops suddenly. He puts his hands on his thighs, buttocks and chest then turns back towards the house. He says something to Angelica. She shrugs her shoulders, shakes her head and puts the key back into the door. He walks back up to her, bends to kiss her cheek. I notice how tall he is. Much taller than Angelica. He holds her hand, lets their fingers slip slowly apart and steps backwards into the house. I rest my spade against the garden fence. This is my chance. Angelica lights a cigarette, holds it to her lips and breathes deeply. She bends her neck from side to side, tips her head and allows the smoke to pour back through her nostrils. The grip, the inhalation and the release. Same as always. She looks up and across at me, realises I'm watching. I hold my hand in the air and wave, but she doesn't wave back. Instead she turns to see where her husband is. But he's still inside. She's on her own. Her skirt seems shorter from the front.

'Angelica,' I shout. She looks up and down the empty street, searching for signs of life. Cressington Vale is empty. There's no-one around. Just me and her. 'I need to speak to you.' She turns around to enter the house and run away like Benny. I shout again before she can open the door. 'I'm not going anywhere.' My voice is clear and confident. I've been practising, repeating my lines in the mirror. I know exactly what I'm going to say. Angelica stands with her back to me. She's thinking about it. Slowly she turns around, folds her arms and starts walking. Her skirt is green and black tartan with thin gold stripes at the hem. Double yellow lines. I try not to look at her legs. She crosses the road and stands beside me, the fence between us. Her fingernails painted red, blue, red, blue, red.

'What do you want?' she says.

'Good morning.'

'What do you want?'

'It's about Georgina. I want to make things

clear. As you know, she's very ill at the moment. It's her preference that she receives care from people that she knows and trusts. Unfortunately, her condition has not improved as we would have liked. So please, Angelica, help us.'

'I've told you, Gordon.'

'I'm begging you.'

'Did you practice that speech?'

'We can work as a team. We can use the manual. You know that I know what I'm doing. She'll start improving in no time.'

'See, I don't think you do know what you're doing. In fact I don't think you have any idea at all. Your plan didn't work. It's wrong, cruel and probably illegal. She needs professional help.'

'I can't let that happen.'

'Why? Why not?'

'It's too late. It's not what she wants.'

'It's not up to her. It's your decision.'

Angelica's husband is leaving the house. I can see him over her shoulder. The collar of her black fluffy-cuffed coat. Flecked with dandruff. He closes the door and walks to the end of the drive. He smiles across the street at me. I smile back and Angelica turns around. Someone else is coming. It's Benny. He's walking towards us on the opposite side of the road. He's carrying a plastic bag and holding hands with a girl who looks younger than he does. Her hair is short and her cheeks are red. She's wearing Benny's jacket. He reaches the gate at the end of his garden and looks across at Angelica. He smiles and nods, lifts and shows us their fingers linked. He does the same to her husband.

'I swear I'll tell him everything.' Angelica turns to face me. 'And I know about the footballs. It was you and him. You were working together. You were laughing at me.'

Benny opens his door and disappears into the house. Her husband is shaking his keys and walking towards us. He's wearing jeans and a suit jacket with a t-shirt underneath. It looks ridiculous. I start to raise my arm, but Angelica reaches over the fence and grips my elbow. She squeezes tight and digs her fingernails into my skin. The pain is short, sharp and only lasts a second. But it takes me by surprise.

'Hello,' says her husband. 'Kids, eh? Who was that?'

'That was no-one. This is Gordon. Gordon, this is Michael.' He offers me his hand to shake. His grip is stronger than mine. It hurts my knuckles. Angelica is smiling, but it's not her real smile. I know what her real smile looks like. Teeth and fillings. Lines from her eyes at the corners. She shuffles her feet and stands by his side. She puts her arm around his waist.

'Beautiful day, isn't it?' he says. 'Sunshine and snow.'

'Very nice,' I reply.

'Perfect for a drive.'

'Where are you going?'

'We don't know yet, do we?' He looks at Angelica, but she doesn't respond. She's too busy glaring at me and tapping her toe on the pavement. He puts his hand on her neck, squeezes her shoulders and lets his fingers run the length of her back. They come to rest on her hip. It's highly inappropriate. I try not to watch.

'Well, it should be nice. Just the two of you.'

'Actually, we're picking David up on the way.'

'David?'

'Angelica's son. It's his birthday tomorrow. We're taking him out for lunch.'

'Oh, I see.' I look at Angelica. Her expression doesn't change. I look back at her husband. 'I didn't know she had children.'

'Yes, he's a grand lad.'

'How old is he?'

'He'll be seventeen.'

'Really?'

'They grow up quickly, don't they?'

I want to hate him. I want to tell him about his wife. That she's spent the last three weeks watching another man paint pictures with his eyes closed. His name's Benny, and he's not really a man, he's a boy. He's the same age as her son. Not your son, her son. We watch him together. Last thing at night. First hours of morning. And that's just the half of it. She kissed his lips and broke his heart. Goodness knows what else.

'I haven't got children myself,' I say. He lifts his eyebrows and offers me his sympathy. His condolences. Angelica stops glaring. She looks away and down the street. She rolls her eyes.

'Come on,' she says. 'We need to get going.'

'Absolutely. Nice to meet you, Gordon.' He takes his arm from her hip and goes to shake my hand again. But I don't respond. I pick up my spade and think about Angelica. The day she moved in. The trip to my parents. The nights with Benny. I watch her reach out, take Michael's outstretched hand and pull him away. He looks embarrassed.

'Nice to meet you too,' I say. He ignores me. They turn in unison and walk towards the car. It's lights flash twice. He opens the passenger door for Angelica. She bends down, ducks under his arm and makes herself comfortable. She drags the seatbelt across her chest and Michael climbs in next to her. They reverse up and into Don's drive, check the street for traffic, pull out and away from me. I look up at sky, the patches of snow on the rooftops. Cressington Vale is silent, apart from the sound of a dull thud, somewhere in the distance. Some kind of banging. It could be the machinery. The lorries. The dual carriageway. But no, it's Benny, standing on a chair in his bedroom, hammering hooks to the wall, at last replacing his curtains.

Yesterday's news

Angelica is leaving Cressington Vale. It's official. Fifteen minutes ago a white van pulled up outside her house. It had pink dice hanging from the rear view mirror. Snow on its roof and bonnet. A man got out and opened the doors at the back. He was wearing a shirt and tie under a pair of orange overalls. I watched him in Angelica's garden, hammering the sign into the ground. I waited for him to finish. To knock on her door and show her what he'd done. But it didn't happen. He just sauntered back to the van, fetched another sign. He dragged it along the pavement to Don Donald's house, stood in his flowerbed, repeated the process. Then he got back inside the van, sat in the driver's seat and removed his overalls. Drove away. I looked at the two signs. One said, 'To Let', the other said, 'For Sale'.

I'm now standing in my back garden. My files are piled in front of me. I brought them down from the loft this morning and placed them into stacks. They are taller than I am. A mountain in the snow on the lawn. Everything is here. K is for Kipling. B is for

Benny. A is for Angelica. There's only one file left to add. My manual. Our lifeline. I position it at the foot of the nearest stack. I reach into my pocket and take out a box of matches. They are long and thin and perfect for bonfires. I open the box by pushing one end, take out a match and strike it. There is a spark and a flicker of life. Then it settles. Glows amber and red in my fingers.

I pause to think of Georgina.

I picture her in hospital. Dying in a care home.

And hope that God intervenes.

Zero tolerance

I'm in the kitchen making tea, waiting for Angelica. It's four o'clock in the afternoon. She arrived home half an hour ago having spent the night elsewhere. I was behind the curtain in the living room when Michael dropped her off. I watched her kiss him goodbye and stand on the pavement as he waved and drove away, his arm through the sunroof, his fingers twirling. Angelica tiptoed from the pavement to her door. Her folded arms and small steps. She was laughing. About something from last night. Something just for her. I waited until she was inside before I made my way to the kitchen. I opened the fridge, sliced a piece of angel cake and placed it on the table. Three separate layers of sponge: pink, white and yellow, each divided by cream. I put my coat around my shoulders, picked up the cake and stepped outside. The air was cold, crisp and stung my gums. I walked to the end of the garden, opened the gate and crossed the road. I checked Angelica's windows. She wasn't watching. She was busy somewhere else. Getting changed or making dinner. I walked to her door, reached into my pocket and took out my notepad and pen. I ripped a page from the pad, folded it in half and dropped it on her doorstep. I placed the cake on top of the note, rattled the letterbox twice, turned and ran away.

★   ★   ★

'I thought you wouldn't come.'

Angelica is here. She's sitting at the kitchen table with green fingernails and wet hair. She's drinking tea and eating cake. I want to ask her how the birthday meal went. Where did they end up going? Tell me more about David. What are his hobbies? What school does he go to? What's it like to have children? It really doesn't matter. She'll never tell me now.

'What made you change your mind?' she says.

I pull out a chair and sit down opposite. I think about answering her question with some questions of my own. Like how would she react if it happened to her husband? What does she think it would feel like to feed him with a spoon? Rub lotion on his bedsores? Empty his commode? I put my elbow on the table and rest my chin on my fist. I look across the table at Angelica. She's not wearing make-up.

'You were right,' I say. 'She needs to be in hospital. It's too much.'

'Gordon, it is too much. Too much for anyone.'

'Maybe. She'd been getting better.'

She bites her lip and shakes her head. I can see the veins in her hands and the lines around her eyes. I want to know about Michael. Is he younger than me? How much did his car cost? What did he *really* forgive you for? She threads her fingers through the handle of her mug, stands up and walks over to the window. She puts her hand to her head and covers her eyes. She looks tired. Upset. Like she might be ready to cry. Then she takes her hand away. I'm right, she's crying. Not much, but enough for me to notice.

'Shall I make the phone call?' she says. I look at the clock on the oven. It's almost ten to five. The last of the daylight is fading away. I put my hands on the edge of the table and use my heels to move the chair.

'I need to speak to Georgina,' I say. 'I need to tell her what's happening.'

'Will she understand?'

'Of course.'

'Shall I wait down here?'

'Yes. How long will it take them to get here?'

'I'm not sure. It depends. Fifteen minutes?'

'That's fine. You can phone while I'm upstairs. It's in the living room. You'll have to plug it in.' Angelica nods at me. She can't believe how calm I am. She thought that I'd be different. I smile and shrug my shoulders. 'What else can we do?'

I open the door and walk to the hall. Georgina's case is at the foot of the stairs. It's her hospital case. It's covered in signatures, signed by the nurses who helped her the first time. I showed it to Angelica when she arrived. She seemed impressed. Inside the case are Georgina's slippers, for when they get her walking. A list of favourite foods, for when she starts to eat again. And her best nightdress, to help her feel at home. I put my hand on the banister, turn and climb the stairs.

★ ★ ★

I'm sitting on the chair next to Georgina's bed. I can see the sky through the gap in the curtain. It tapers up and over rooftops. Red to blue. Blue to black. I've been holding her hand, mopping her brow and massaging her fingers. It's supposed to stop them curling, but she's too far gone already. Her hand is like a claw. She's changing shape in front of me. Exhausted and half paralysed. I've been upstairs for eight minutes. Only seven more to go before they come to take her away. I stroke her arm with the back of my hand. Her skin is dry and lifeless. She won't get any better. There's nothing they can do.

'Georgina,' I whisper. She doesn't respond. I let my fingertips rest on her cheek and comb her hair behind her ear. I watch her eyelids flickering. She's in another world. On another planet. I can hear Angelica. She's back in the kitchen, clearing cups and making noise. Keeping herself busy. I listened to her talking on the phone to the hospital. The emergency services. She was calm and collected, softly spoken, brief and to the point. She told them what the problem was and answered all their questions. Then silence, for a while. She gave them our address.

'Georgina,' I say, louder than before but not enough to make a difference. A strip of light shines through from the landing. I think about it waking her up, hurting her eyes should they open. But it's never going to happen. Not any more. We made our decision together. Last week before the snow came. I held her hand and asked her questions.

Prepared a plan of action. And now the time has come. I put my hands on my knees, stand up straight and slowly turn around. I untie the cushion and remove it from the chair. It feels warm from where I've been sitting. It's ripped along the seam. I turn again to face Georgina. My beautiful wife. This is what she wanted. This was our decision. I shut my eyes and count the seconds. Ten. Twenty. Thirty.

Angelica is coming. I can hear the crockery, the floorboards and her heels on the stairs. I reattach the cushion and sit down on the chair. She knocks on the door, peers through the gap and shuffles into the room. She looks across at me, then down at Georgina. I'm here to say my goodbyes. Explain to her what's happening. Angelica stands beside me, offers me some chocolate cake, asks me if I'm ready. But I don't answer properly. I never answer properly. I sit and I stare.

'Did you know the Russians have a special word for light blue?' I say.

She looks away. Sips her tea. Shakes her head.

'Just get on with it,' she replies. 'Before your drink gets cold.'

Other titles published by
The House of Ulverscroft:

THE CHRISTMAS SPIRITS

Whitley Strieber

George Moore is a modern day Scrooge, mean with his money, his time and his sympathies. A futures trader who drives his staff hard, George won't even let his assistant go home on Christmas Eve so she can look after her son. But on his way home that night, odd things start to happen . . . When he finally arrives back in his apartment, George is accosted by his old mentor in trading and greed, Bill Hill. Bill warns George that he will receive three visitors who will give him his only chance at salvation. But the thing is, Bill Hill is dead . . .